SPAM

STORIES · POEMS · ANECDOTES · MEMORIES

SWitCH

SPAM

Short stories, poems, anecdotes and memories from SWit'CH

Copyright and Ordering

Copyright © 2024 by authors and SWit'CH

All rights reserved. This book or any portion thereof may not be reproduced or used in any manner whatsoever without the express written permission of the authors except for the use of brief quotations in a book review or scholarly journal.

First Edition: 2024
ISBN: 9798879706468

Swinton Writers in t'Critchley Hub
Manchester
United Kingdom

Email: switchswinton@gmail.com

Website: http://switchswinton.epizy.com

Ordering Information:

Published with Amazon KDP.
Available through Amazon and good book distributors or directly from SWit'CH by email: switchswinton@gmail.com

All rights reserved.

Table of Contents

SWit'CH 6
SPAM 7
   Stories
   Poems
   Anecdotes
   Memories
Pop the Kettle On! 9
   Caroline Barden
Worth Sharing 10
   Graham E Walker
A Christmas Cracker. 12
   Judith Barrie
Castle Grimwall 17
   Judith Barrie
Precious More than Rubies 29
   Judith Barrie
A Cat's Nine Lives 40
   Rosemary Swift
Mayday... Mayday 43
   Rosemary Swift
Violet the Shrink 45
   Rosemary Swift
Gerald's Dream 47
   Catherine Grant-Salmon
Masquerade 52
   Catherine Grant-Salmon
Bah Humbug 56
   Catherine Grant-Salmon
Couch to Romance 61
   Catherine Grant-Salmon
An Interesting Experience 66
   Catherine Grant-Salmon
The Jewellery Box 69
   Catherine Grant-Salmon
Teacup 72
   Catherine Grant-Salmon

DAVID'S SYSTEM 74
   Catherine Grant-Salmon
THE MEETING 76
   Lorraine Tattersall
POPPY'S TONGUE 80
   Lorraine Tattersall
GHOST'S STORY. 83
   Pauline Mitchell
ABANDONED 85
   Veronica Scotton
FRANK THE PAINTER 88
   Veronica Scotton
IBRAHIM 91
   Veronica Scotton
THE SYSTEM 94
   Veronica Scotton
THE BEST BRANDY AND GIN MINCEMEAT EVER 96
   Veronica Scotton
CONJOINED TWINS 100
   Veronica Scotton
INNOCENCE LOST 106
   Colin Balmer
FRANK THE PAINTER 108
   Colin Balmer
SUE FINDS LOVE. 110
   Colin Balmer
PLAGUE IN THE VILLAGE 112
   Caroline Barden
SEEDS. 117
   Warren Davies
FEAR 119
   Warren Davies
DEMENTIA (SLIDING AND SLIPPING) 121
   Warren Davies
HEALTH AND SAFETY 123
   Warren Davies
THE COMMITTEE (HS2) 125
   Warren Davies

A FORGOTTEN MAN 127
    Warren Davies
TIME 129
    Warren Davies
THE TRAIN 131
    Warren Davies
POPPIES 132
    Sylvia Edwards
WHERE NO BIRDS SING 134
    Sylvia Edwards
ODE TO LIFE, POSITIVITY AND WRITING 136
    Sylvia Edwards
MY 'GO TO' FRIEND 139
    Christine Barwood
LITTLE RED POPPY 140
    Paul Hallows.
I'M LONELY 141
    Rosemary Swift
ODE TO OSTRICHISM 142
    Mary Young
OLD AGE 144
    Paul Hallows
WASTE 145
    Veronica Scotton
THREE PEBBLES 148
    © *Graham E Walker*
THE LOAN SHARK 149
    Veronica Scotton
RIPPED JEANS 153
    Paul Hallows
HAVE YOU GOT…? 155
    Catherine Grant-Salmon
MATHEMATICAL EVOLUTION 157
    Colin Balmer
GLASS HOUSES 158
    Colin Balmer
RASPUTIN. SIR! 159
    Paul Hallows

ONCE UPON A TIME IN SALFORD 160
    Bernie Shaw
LIFE'S BETTER ON A HOUSEBOAT 162
    Rosemary Swift
CORINTHIAN LADIES 164
    Rosemary Swift
MUSIC AND DANCE WITH DEMENTIA 166
    Chris Vickers
WHERE ARE THEY? 170
    Lorraine Tattersall
OTHER PUBLICATIONS BY SWIT'CH 172

SWIT'CH

The social group of creative writers referred to as SWit'CH, was formed in 2015 at Age UK Swinton community hub – Swinton Writers in t'Critchley Hub

Our aims are to provide an environment for the local community for recreational, social or educational enjoyment of members' creative writing.

To support each other and strengthen community spirit by co-operative involvement in creative writing.

To cover associated disciplines, including but not limited to, illustrating, editing, proofing, reading, publishing and distributing.

To promote and encourage equal opportunities within the group.

To work closely with other groups having compatible aims and objectives.

Activities of our group are writing, reading and publishing members' works, including but not limited to fiction and non-fiction, stories, reports, poetry and plays.

Projects will take into consideration the needs and priorities of local people.

Tasks will be set to give maximum variety and challenge.

The work of SWit'CH will take into account how it can be used for the greater benefit of the community in general and not-for-profit organisations whenever possible.

Membership is open to all irrespective of age, race, ability, gender, political or religious belief.

Writers and non-writing support service providers will have equal status and equal rights.

All members will be required to act reasonably with good manners, deference and common sense paramount.

Email: switchswinton@gmail.com

SPAM

STORIES
POEMS
ANECDOTES
MEMORIES

This collection of the works of SWit'CH has been collated to showcase the variety and skills of the dynamic writers in and around Swinton, Salford.

The sources and prompts for some of the creations are included to demonstrate what stimulates our creativity, whether in-session exercises, 'homeworks' or personal major projects.

As you read through these and further writings from the published works listed in the appendix, we hope you understand our commitment to the English language and the beautiful flowers of the pen that we have nurtured.

Whilst we don't aim to be controversial, we are, nonetheless, not averse to provocation as a stimulus for reasonable minds.

Please, please, let us have some feedback to reinforce our vanity publishing for the future.

Most of our works are available through Amazon, and the Amazon KDP service was crucial to the publication of this collection. Search SWit'CH (including the apostrophe) to find them. Add a few lines of reader notes to the Amazon website.

STORIES
POP THE KETTLE ON!

CAROLINE BARDEN

> Writing Challenge:
> Picked from magazine snippets

It took a long time to move house. Long hours of tramping the streets with frozen toes, feeling the disappointment of yet another damp squib of a house, followed by seemingly endless waiting on a station platform for a train to take us home while the wind whipped our hair and bit into our cheeks.

Time marched on relentlessly with no end in sight, but then in January, after months of searching, there was a rail strike which put us in a tight spot by effectively stopping all our viewings for the duration. So when a house in the listings caught our eye we asked our son and daughter-in-law to view it instead.

The message came back later that day, "We like it. It's a safe haven just right for you. Go for it!"

The next day we crossed our fingers very tight and made an offer unseen.

Luckily, we liked it too when we saw it a week later. I knew we would: it was full of sunshine and the layout was good.

The house had been very neglected, and I think it was longing for us as much as we longed for it. When we were asked "Will you do it up before you move in?" the answer was always "No, we'll be moving in as soon as we can."

Less than two months later we had the keys and that was when our close relationship with various builders and plumbers began.

We loved them all as they transformed the house into our home. From the shy quiet ones to the noisy ones who turned their radio on loud enough to hear above the drilling, they all did a wonderful job.

But to them we were just another workplace until, of course, we said the magic words, "I'll go and pop the kettle on!" and then they would sup sweet tea and eat chocolate biscuits with broad smiles that lit up the room, and all was right with the world.

WORTH SHARING

Graham E Walker

What's worth Sharing? Quality Street chocolates or Cadbury's snaps maybe?

Passing a chocolate (or two) to someone is a gesture of kindness perhaps, a peace offering or simply because someone is next to you when you are having your chocolate and it could be a chance to glabber. Worth sharing?

J M Barrie's play 'Quality Street' first made its stage appearance in 1901. The play takes place in the Napoleonic War period. Two of the protagonists, sister's Phoebe and Susan, attend a 'high society' school. Phoebe, fed up of her chaperoned lifestyle invents a flighty character in 'Lilly' and shared her 'secret identity' with Susan. Captain Valentine BROWN, who initially travels to see the sisters and it's Phoebe's belief that the Captain would ask for her hand. However, the information shared is that Captain Brown is off to war. Worth sharing?

Sharing something valuable can be mutually 'worthy' I guess, or can it? Is it admirable, is it valuable, is it worthwhile? What are the outcomes of sharing something? Does it give your brain a positive impact? Does it trigger your dopamine? Does it improve your mood? Does giving someone a portion of your insight help? Do you feel better after offloading your information? What drove you to share? Does the person on the receiving end appreciate what you have shared? Why did you share? Worth sharing?

If you don't share things are you stingy, miserly, parsimonious even? Did you gain anything from not sharing? Take the pastry, give it a birl and decide what needs sharing and why, and take the sole off someone's shoes? What value are your words or are they worth their weight in burnt copper? Worth sharing?

Are you in fear of being rejected or judged? Then keep quiet, but then, maybe don't. Are you looking to gain attention with your statements? Are you looking for admiration and gratification? Could you be in jeopardy of sharing lashes? Did you think before you

STORIES

spoke? Or are you the tallawah of the team, the omniscient one? Are you the all sharing extrovert? Do you pour your heart out to a kind listening ear and unburden your tensions on them? Worth sharing?

Do you share with your young your valuable time and experience? Do you leave them to fend all alone? Do they make friends well? Do they share playtime activities with your oversight, do they compromise well as mentee's, do you seek something back from your promulgation techniques? Do you help them unfold, do you help them dilate with the circulation of your wisdom? Worth sharing?

It's not about being the best, its not about sharing being always caring. A convivial approach may work and when you know you are capable of something you could stop worrying maybe and start amazing yourself, and possibly others. We may make a living from what we know and what we have, however, may make a life with what we give. Life is too short to hold grudges, let it go, because in the end we may only regret the chances and opportunities we didn't take so use the reservoirs of your potential in the best ways possible and consider conveying your feelings, your thoughts, your ideas, your insight. So give someone the rub of your thumb instead of giving it away with a pound of tea.

Is it really worth sharing?

A CHRISTMAS CRACKER.
Or An Endless Pantomime with a Happy Ending.
JUDITH BARRIE

'Twas the night before Christmas and three of the clock in the afternoon. The daylight was fading fast, although, in truth, it had never really been light that day. The High Street was a-bustle with excited children, noses pressed to the window of the Old Curiosity Shop with great expectations, while their weary parents were eager to get home and in front of their hearths to enjoy a sup of Christmas cheer.

There was no cheer, however, in the Counting House where Joe Scratchit was crouched over his desk frantically adding up columns of figures, his fingers so numb with cold that he could scarce hold his quill. The fire, meagre at the best of times, had finally expired with a last feeble gasp and there was not a nugget of coal left to stir it into life. His mittens, which had once been gloves when knitted some years before by Mrs Scratchit, gave no comfort and he pulled his threadbare muffler tighter round his neck in an effort to gain a little warmth.

For the umpteenth time, he added up the figures in the vain hope that he had made a miscalculation, but without success. He thought of his wife and brood of children waiting at home with empty bellies, his youngest with the beginnings of the fever which was spreading over the land, like a plague.

He was interrupted from his reverie by a clatter at the door and a booming voice: 'Wake up, Sleepy Joe! I don't pay you fifteen shillings a week to take forty winks every time my back is turned!' Ebenezer Trump swept through the door bringing in with him a flurry of snow, but slightly warmer air.

'Yes, sir,' agreed Joe quietly.

'Well? Have you worked out how much profit I have made this past year? Out with it man! No time for your dillying and dallying!'

Ebenezer Trump was not well regarded by the common folk of the town, on account of his being a tight-fisted, squeezing, wrenching, scraping, clutching, covetous, miserly, curmudgeonly old skin-flint.

Joe Scratchit was quaking in his well-ventilated boots. 'Well, sir...er...'

'Get on with it man! How much profit have I made?' he bellowed. Ebenezer's eyes rested on the gleaming piles of coins on the desk, his ruddy face contorted with greed.

'Well...I think there is a total of seven pounds, seventeen shillings and sixpence ha'penny here, but...'

'Is that all?' Ebenezer thundered. 'What do you mean, *you think*? There must be more than that...'

In truth, the total had been different every time Joe had counted it as he kept getting confused and forgetting the numbers. 'And, er...' he stuttered, 'We owe the coalman nearly two pounds, sir. And, er, the butcher fifteen and fourpence, and your hatter is owed eight pounds ten shillings...'

'Never! Are you telling me that we have no profit?'

'Well, sir, yes...'

'Then you must have counted falsely, you wretch, I have made much profit this year, by a lot! Your report is fake, Joe Scratchit, count it again, you fool!'

Joe looked dismally at the piles of coins on his desk. 'But, sir, I have counted it five times already, and...'

'Well, count it again! And you can re-count it as many times as it takes until you get the right answer!' Ebenezer was becoming purple in the face by now. 'I'm off to get my dinner at the White House Tavern and a cup of hot punch. I want this put right when I get back!'

Ebeneezer stormed out of the door, bringing more snow flurries inside. Joe heaved a sigh of relief. Ebeneezer was due to come up before the beak for fraud and obstruction of official proceeding in the new year, and Joe was hoping for a *very* long sentence. Mind, his own son, Hunter, was in trouble with the peelers for brandishing his flintlock at all and sundry and for failing to pay his taxes.

Joe sighed deeply, then sadly turned back to his task. Forty-two farthings, that made tenpence ha'penny; twenty-six halfpennies, one shilling and a penny; ninety-two pennies, seven shillings and tenpence; thirty thruppenny bits…Oh, no! he was sure there had been thirty-one before. That was even worse. He scrabbled around the floor and found the missing coin stuck in the floorboards by the empty hearth. He could scarce grasp it between his frozen fingers, but by then he'd forgotten the total and had to start again.

Twenty-nine sixpences, fourteen shillings and sixpence; sixteen shillings; forty-one florins, four pounds two shillings and nineteen half-crowns, two pounds seven shillings and sixpence. There was not a single bank note in sight. Joe added it up once more and it came to a different total. He watched mournfully as a robin landed on the windowsill outside and started tweeting.

Ebenezer returned from the tavern two hours later. It was pitch dark outside and the snow was deeper. He was furious when Joe gave him the news. 'Well, I want you back in here tomorrow morning, at seven sharp and you can count it again! I have made a good profit and you are trying to steal it from me!'

'But Mr Trump, sir, it's Christmas morning tomorrow, and my youngest child is sick…'

'Nonsense! Disease is a gift from God! Give him a potion of bleach and he will be fine. But *you* will do my bidding until you get the right answer,' he shouted. 'And you can look for other employment in the New Year, I can easily replace you, Joe Scratchit. People love me and would be glad to work for me for fifteen shillings a week!' And with that, Ebenezer Trump turned on his well-shod foot and stormed off into the night, his well-upholstered coach awaiting him down the street. Joe Scratchit left, stumbling over the step on his way out and falling into the snow. He stood up shakily, then trudged his weary way home to a dry crust and cup of water.

Christmas morning dawned clear and bright, but colder still. Joe Scratchit dragged his weary body back to the Counting House to start another day's work. He counted the heaps of coins again but nothing had changed; there was a different answer every time. At nine o'clock carol singers stood outside the door and he could hear

STORIES

their joyful voices: 'Hark the New York Tribune sings, Glory to Bi - den, our new King...' then they treated him to a merry chorus of 'A Dog in a manger...' He wished he could hand over the piles of coins to them, he wished with all his heart, but he dare not...

It was almost noon when Ebenezer Trump appeared.

'Well, Sleepy Joe? How much profit have I made?'

'None, sir,' Joe said miserably. 'I still reach the same total, and when we've paid...'

'You will pay nothing, Joe Scratchit! And you will be *paid* nothing! I can't wait around here all day! Nigella, my cook, has my Christmas dinner ready and there is a fine plump breast and a meaty thigh waiting for me. Lock the door when you leave and bring me the key tomorrow.' And with that, Ebenezer Trump swept out through the door and back into his carriage.

'Well,' thought Joe, 'his poor deceased uncle Abraham Lincoln will be spinning in his grave to hear such heartlessness.' He sat silent awhile while he tried to remember what he had to do next, then slowly started to put the coins back into the leather bags and tidy his desk. He was lost in reverie when, an hour later, little Stevie Bannon, Ebenezer's servant boy, dashed into the shop, panting in a state of high excitement.

'Mister Joe, sir! Mister Joe, the Master's gone and snuffed it! He choked on a turkey leg and nothing could be done, sir! Too much stuffing, sir, that's what Nigella said. She woz wiv 'im when he croaked it, sir!'

Joe took a half-crown from the leather bag and Stevie's eyes sparkled as he first bit on it, then, satisfied with its authenticity, secreted it in his pocket and skipped off up the road. A broad smile curled on Joe's lips as he remembered something. He opened the bottom drawer in his desk, put his hand right to the back and pulled out a roll of banknotes tied round with a ribbon. Ten bob notes, pound sterling notes and even a couple of fivers. A total of fifty-seven pounds, ten shillings. He had no need to count them, he had done so many times before and written the total on a piece of paper. 'Oh, dear,' he murmured to himself. 'My memory let me down again! I seem to have forgotten these.' So, he put the notes in his pocket, locked up the office and went merrily on his way. 'Yes,' he thought, 'we might have missed the turkey, but for New Year we shall have a fine goose, with roast potatoes. Should we have apple sauce or lashings of gravy? I'll leave that to my dear wife! But we will follow it by a plum pudding smothered in brandy and cream…' He carried on his merry way, whistling.

Strangely, nobody could be bothered to go to Ebenezer Trump's funeral. Even his wife, Melania, was too busy sorting out his off-shore fund accounts, so it was a truly sad affair. But the Scratchit family lived happily ever after.

STORIES
CASTLE GRIMWALL.

JUDITH BARRIE

PART ONE

The kitchens were right at the top of the castle, in the west wing: great, cavernous spaces, with billowing smoke and steam making it difficult to see the frantic action below. The air was thick with the smell of burnt flesh, frying fish, onions and garlic, boiling cabbage and simmering bones, all mixed together in a gut-churning odour. Here were prepared hundreds of meals every day, although no one ever saw, or even knew, who ate them; they were just trundled out on huge trolleys to the lower sections of the castle and never seen again.

Almost a hundred minions worked in the kitchens, although it was difficult to keep track of their numbers, because The Chef, a huge brute of a man, would think nothing of taking a minion by a leg or an arm and throwing him over the battlements to the jagged rocks below if he'd not jumped fast enough in his response to do The Chef's bidding.

The minions did not have names and were only differentiated by the colour of their uniforms: red for meat preparation, green for vegetables, blue for fish and yellow for puddings. Some wore only grey, and these were the lowliest of them all – new recruits that were given the dirtiest, smelliest jobs and were teased mercilessly by the others as they mopped the stinking floors or carried buckets of swill out to the pigs that were penned outside the castle walls. All the minions were the same size, so small that they had to stand on short ladders to reach the top of the gigantic stoves, and it took three or four of them to lift the huge iron cauldrons that gurgled and bubbled, spitting boiling soup onto their tiny, raw hands.

The Chef was busy making his favourite apple fritters, his best copper frying pan full of oil, smoking on the stove. Just as he was about to put in the first fritters, a grey minion, carrying a large bowl of pepper for the venison stew, was deliberately tripped up by a mischievous blue minion. The bowl flew upwards, scattering the pepper in a great cloud, showering the apple fritters.

The empty bowl was catapulted high in the air, somersaulting down to hit the handle of the copper frying pan, tipping it over and causing the boiling oil to pour over the front of The Chef, liberally scalding his lower portions.

He roared like a lion, he bellowed like a bull, screaming out with pain, cursing and yelling at the grey minion:

'You squinty-eyed slimy toad!'

'Son of a fetid dingo's kidney!'

'You mangy shitzu-stirring rodent!'

He seized the grey minion by the scruff of the neck, his little legs dangling.

'You strangulated French food whopper!'

'Congealed plate of dog's vomit!'

'You're a chopper-toting cockroach!'

'Duplicitous dung-beetle!'

'Menu-blasting bigoted lizard!'

'You are a bumbling, bombastic booby...' he screeched.

And all the while the pepper floated down like a toxic cloud of grey dust. The Chef flung the grey minion to the other end of the kitchen, through the billowing smoke and steam, where he landed, head first, in a vat of pancake batter.

And then The Chef started to sneeze...

PART TWO

The seven hunters trudged through the thick snow back to the castle, their nine hounds prancing by their sides, the scent of the two wild boars tantalising in their nostrils.

They had been out since dawn and had walked miles through the deserted forest in search of food, but all they had found were the

STORIES

tracks of the two scrawny beasts whose carcasses were now hanging from the thick wooden poles carried by the men.

Poles thick enough to carry a stag, but almost all signs of life had gone to ground that bitter winter, and by the time The Chef had finished with these skinny boars, the men would be lucky to get the bones to chew on.

The castle reared up before them in the dusk like a set of jagged teeth, much like the mountains all around them. The snow was falling faster now, and deeper where it had drifted up against the castle walls. The weary men could scarcely wait to peel off their sodden clothes and sit with a hot drink and perhaps a bite to eat in front of the fire. There might even be some scraps from the kitchens – or perhaps not.

The gatekeeper had lowered the drawbridge in readiness for their return and they held their lanterns high as the gathering gloom pressed down over the land.

They were fifty yards from their destination when they heard a mighty roar, followed by a yelp and, kicking and screaming, a small body was hurled from the battlements high above, falling like a feather onto the snow then sinking slowly out of sight.

'The Chef! Another minion!' Albrus lifted his lantern higher and the men waded through the snow to see the body. The hounds bounded over and by the time the men reached the tiny grey minion the dogs were frantically licking him from head to foot.

'Don't let them eat me,' cried the petrified minion. 'Please...Don't let them eat me!'

Albrus roughly pulled the dogs away. 'God's blood!' he cried to the others, 'He looks as if he's covered in custard!'

The men roared with laughter. 'Let the dogs enjoy their pudding!' Bruegon cried. 'They'll get naught else tonight!'

'Please! I beg of you, don't let the dogs eat me! I will do *anything* but don't let the dogs rip me apart!'

The dogs, having licked up most of the pancake batter, now started tearing at his clothes. The grey minion yelped as they tore into his flesh in their eagerness. Albrus looked into the little man's fearful blue eyes and called the dogs away. 'What is your name?' he asked.

'I...I don't have a name. I'm a grey minion. We don't have names.'

'I shall call you Min,' said Albrus. 'And it's your good fortune that the snow is so deep tonight and that I might have a need of a willing fellow.'

He pulled Min out of the snow and tossed him over his shoulder with more ease than if he had carried a dead fox. It was not uncommon for the hunters to find these tiny bodies dashed on the rocks below the kitchens high above, and Albrus usually let his hounds have their way, but this one was unscathed by his fall into the deep snow and it would be a shame to waste an eager slave.

The gatekeeper, roused from his slumbers, looked suspiciously at the ragged, bleeding bundle over Albrus's shoulders, but Min lay limp as if dead.

'I will feed the hounds in the yard tonight,' Albrus said. 'It's not a fit night for even a dog to be out there.' The gatekeeper nodded sleepily and started to wind the drawbridge back into its place for the night, shutting out the bitter wind and chill.

The sounds of merriment tumbled out of the Great Hall as the men walked wearily past towards the crumbling tower where they lived. Lord Daltild was feasting again, as he did every night; a thousand candles burning, a great fire roaring, his boards groaning with dishes of exquisite delicacy. The Lady Mellissa would be there, nibbling on dainty morsels, sipping the finest ruby red wine. Rumour had it that the lady hated Lord Daltild, her father, who terrorised her ladies-in-waiting and was, even now, said to be arranging a suitable husband for her.

Albrus thought tenderly of her long hair, as black as any jet and sleek as a raven's wing; her slender figure; the grace when she walked. He had seen her arms once, on the hottest of days when she was resting by the lily-pool in the gardens, the creamy skin and beautiful hands, the fingers so long and shapely, but she had blushed at the sight of him walk past and her ladies swiftly sheltered her from his sight.

STORIES

The boars were handed over to a couple of ragged scullions who quickly conveyed them up the winding stone stairs to the kitchens high above. They knew they would get a hearty clout from The Chef, ever disappointed with whatever was brought to him. The huntsmen trudged along the damp and crumbling passageway to their turret on the east wing of the castle. At least there would be a fire waiting and some kind of food. And the plump, warm arms of Lettice, if she was in a good mood.

The little minion had remained lifeless and when he was laid down on a pallet in front of the fire, he merely moaned. The men pulled off their boots and drank deeply of the warm ale.

'What's that?' demanded Lettice, viewing the minion with distaste.

'He's our new servant, Lettie, we're getting rid of you!' Albrus said, teasing.

'Well, it needs a good washing!' she replied, her brow furrowed.

Albrus seized Lettie round her ample waist and gave her a squeeze. 'Take him away and find some clouts for him,' he said. 'And give him a bite to eat.' So she took Min by the hand, rather taken by the little fellow with his yellow hair and frightened blue eyes. She led him to her chamber where she washed and fed him, then dressed him in a clean tunic and hose that had once belonged to her brother.

The night enfolded the castle in its icy black arms and all was still within. But not quiet, as the castle bell tolled the midnight hour. Min was snuggled down on his pallet before the dying embers, welcoming the warmth from the hounds as they edged closer round him, snuffling and shuffling and whimpering in their slumbers. The hunters were snoring and grunting in their sleep, but none so loud and stridently as Sir Daltild, who lay on his back, covered by fine silken sheets. He was dreaming of a great haunch of venison, served with cherry pottage and mulled wine. Amiria, the distraught handmaiden took a glance at the great lump of blubber beside her in the bed and seized the opportunity to slip silently out of the chamber and flee, barefoot, down the corridors to safety in her own chamber next to her Lady's.

In the frozen chapel, Sir Daltild's wife lay entombed in black marble and cared no longer for her husband's infidelities. Death had long ago put an end to her pain and suffering. *Requiesce in pace.*

The beadsman, his fingers too numb to tell his five and forty rosary beads, offered up his mumbled prayers, his frosted breath rising heavenwards like incense with his words: *Deus meus, ex toto corde poenitet me omnium…*

In her dismal chamber at the top of the highest tower, the lovely Lady Mellissa stood by the opened latticed window, oblivious to the icy blasts. She gazed out over the snow-covered slopes, over the craggy peaks and naked forests down to the sea. The wind had scattered the ragged clouds and the full moon shone brightly. A lone owl was flying across the sky back to its ancient belfry, silhouetted against the yellow orb. It let out a single mournful cry: *hoo, hoo, hoooooo…*

A tear ran down our Lady's cheek as she listened to her loyal servant Amiria sobbing in the next chamber, and she shuddered at the thought of her wicked father and his evil deeds. He had lately arranged her marriage to Sir Osbert Stridbeck. She had heard tell of Sir Osbert's cruelty and uncouth ways and dreaded the years ahead of her. She was in her nineteenth year and her life seemed already over. It would be a fate worse than death, some said. She leaned over the casement to see the frozen ground below and putting her slender palms together prayed for the strength to hurl herself down to the rocks below. But the snow was too deep yet and might cushion her fall, and her father's wrath would know no bounds if she were left living. When the snow had gone, then… then she would commit herself to the Lord's mercy.

She pulled the silken robe around her slender body and padded over the rushes, her tender feet blue-veined and icy, to finally lay her troubled head down on her bed with its hangings of gold and crimson woven cloth, her heart cleft in two.

And on his pallet, far down below, Min turned over, restless, dreaming dreams of sweet revenge.

STORIES

The snow melted away from the land and, slowly, the buds fattened on the boughs. The hunters went out every day and brought back rabbits, deer and geese. Spring was approaching and little Min was always there at hand when the men came back, weary, cold and ravenous at night. Always at hand and ready to run any errand, fetch and carry, perform any task for Albrus, his saviour.

Venturing back to the kitchens, unrecognisable in his new garb, he spoke to some of the grey minions, still slaving for The Chef, whose temper had become even more brutal and there wasn't a soul that worked for him that wouldn't rejoice to see him dead and buried.

'But it would take twenty grown men to do the job!' a grey minion complained to Min.

'Wait and see, little friends,' whispered Min. 'Wait and see!'

The time had come for Sir Daltild to announce the betrothal of his lovely Lady Mellissa to Sir Osbert Stridbeck. There was to be the most splendid banquet in his honour on the first day of spring. For weeks The Chef was instructed about the dishes to be served, the special wines to be offered and Sir Daltild fussed and fretted over every detail.

With only a single child – and that a daughter – it was essential that a good marriage was made to unite his daughter to a family that was prosperous and influential at court. The Stridbeck family owned many rich and fertile lands across the sea and it mattered not that Sir Osbert was an old man and Mellissa was distraught with grief. She prostrated herself at her father's feet and pleaded with him to release her from this marriage, but he would hear none of it. 'You must do your duty, child!' he thundered. And on the advice of her old nurse, Agnes, the lattice window in her room was barred over to prevent any 'accidents'.

Albrus was likewise distraught. 'How can a father treat his own daughter like a piece of meat, to be sold to the highest bidder?' he shouted.

'Come,' said Bruegon, 'Mellissa is uncommon fair, but she has to be married soon to someone, and if she could choose any man that took her fancy, my friend, she would not choose you,'

Albrus put his head in his hands in despair. 'That I know, that I know! But to have to suffer that monster in her bed... I hear tales of his depravities that would shock the hardiest of men.'

Min timidly approached Albrus and said: 'I think I may know a way, Master. I have friends still in the kitchens and it might be possible to furnish Sir Osbert with a potion that would put him into a sleep from which he would never awaken.'

'Make close the door,' Albus instructed Bruegon. Then he turned to Min, his eyes glittering. 'Tell me more, my little friend...'

The preparations for the feast carried on at a frantic pace. Every effort must be made to impress Sir Osbert. Mellissa's nurse, Agnes, pleaded with Sir Daltild that his daughter had been refusing to eat her food and was naught but skin and bone. 'Her clothes are hanging from her, she is like a walking skeleton,' she said.

'Well fatten her up!' he yelled.

Even Albrus noticed how unhappy Mellissa was as she wandered round the castle like a wraith. She was, indeed, as skinny as a fox in January and her hair had lost its lustrous raven's sheen. Albrus gave Min a handful of silver coins in a leather purse to make payment to any minion that would assist in their plan, begging that he should be spared the details until the deed was done.

It was the custom, at such an occasion as a betrothal, that fragrant jellies were to be fashioned in wines both red and white and decorated with the crests of the two parties. Sir Osbert would be served with the jelly bearing the coat of arms of Sir Daltild, and on eating it would show his acceptance of Sir Daltild's daughter as his wife.

It was an easy matter for Min to visit the old crone who lived in the cave under the castle walls and buy the black berries of the deadly nightshade plant. She took the silver coins greedily into her outstretched, wrinkled palm and gave Min a small bag containing the shiny black berries. 'Enough to kill twenty horses,' she said, her eyes twinkling. 'And here's something to flavour a drink for my

STORIES

Lord, if he should find his throat becoming a little dry. We wouldn't want to make him suffer too long, eh?' She pressed a twist of parchment into Min's hands and started to cackle. He looked at it doubtfully. 'A little hemlock to speed him on his way!' Her laughter echoed round the cave.

The sounds of her mirth followed Min back inside the castle walls. He had concealed the poison in his tunic and lost no time in conveying it to his minion friends in the kitchen.

'Can we use some of it for The Chef?' they begged.

'All in good time my little friends, all in good time. Now, you know what to do...?'

The morning of the feast arrived and Sir Daltild paced back and forth over the stone flags of the Great Hall. Every care had been taken to welcome the honoured guests. The Hall was bestrewn with garlands of fresh herbs and blossoms, the boards were covered in the finest white linens, the serving minions all garbed in the brightest blue uniforms stood prepared, while the guardsmen, halberds at the ready, shuffled uneasily, weighted down in their suits of armour. The party of guests was espied from the battlements some miles in the distance and the trumpeters stood ready to welcome them.

In the kitchens, the pace had become frantic, The Chef's voice booming as dish after dish was conveyed to the banquet tables. The billows of steam and smoke had been such that Min's accomplices had had no further need of disguise in slipping the deadly black berries into the red-wine jelly, along with the raspberries, blackberries and red currents that it was stuffed with. The top was carefully dressed by The Chef himself with an oak tree fashioned from angelica and nuts set on a portcullis fashioned from candied fruits. This was the crest of Sir Daltild and was intended to represent protection, virtue and strength.

The crest of Sir Oswald was a much more lively affair, with a dragon, an axe and an arrow set on argent, to demonstrate his military prowess.

The lord's party finally streamed over the drawbridge and into the courtyard, dozen after dozen. They were led by Sir Osbert in all his armoured splendour and he was flanked by his finest two young knights, Sir Bracy and Sir Roland. There was a flurry of minions who ran to take charge of the horses and the guests were brought to meet their host.

Mellissa, watching the arrival from her tower, swooned at the sight of them and Agnes had to force drops of wine between her lips to revive her. 'Courage, courage, my little one. Women have faced worse fates!' But Mellissa could think of none.

When she was finally brought down to the Great Hall, the feast was ready to begin and the guests were being entertained by Hildebrand, the dwarf. At the sight of the tables stacked with enormous pies, silver platters piled high with great slabs of meat and fish, a suckling pig and glistening capons, Mellissa almost swooned again. Agnes had spent many hours preparing her, braiding her hair into the most elaborate coiffeur. She had padded out her gown in the pretence of flesh on her bones and painted her eyes with antimony to darken her brows and lashes. She reddened her bloodless lips with a mixture of cochineal and gum Arabic. There had been no need of whitening her face, and, indeed, nothing could disguise her great beauty.

Sir Osbert's first glimpse of his intended bride clearly pleased him, his reptilian lips curling into a fiendish smile. Mellissa, however, was repulsed by this wrinkled, fat old man, but was comforted by the thought that he might not have many years left to him on this earth, and then she could be free.

She was seated at the board and various sweetmeats were piled onto her platter. She drank deeply from the goblet of wine in the expectation that it might dull her senses, but nervously dallied with the piecrust until it was reduced to crumbs on her plate.

Sir Daltild, having gorged himself with every manner of sweetmeat, made the sign that they were ready for the ceremonial jellies to be served. The red jelly with his own crest was put before him and Sir Osbert's white jelly set down likewise. There was a tense moment when Sir Daltild, his greedy eyes on the appetising concoction before him, almost plunged his spoon into the quivering delight, but a discreet cough from his table companion reminded him of his duties, and the jellies were duly exchanged as a symbol of the joining of their noble families.

STORIES

Mellissa blushed deeply at the sight of her future husband spooning great dollops of the fruit-laden red confection into his mouth, much in the manner of a wild boar rooting for truffles. When Sir Osbert finally pushed the near-empty dish aside he let out a huge belch and called for another slice of pie. But it was only a few minutes later when he suddenly seemed to have had his fill and, sweeping the dishes aside, clutched at his throat in some distress. He tried to stand, but staggered to the side where he was supported by his knights.

'I cannot see!' he shouted. 'What have you done to me?'

Being too heavy for the two knights to support, he was laid down on the stone floor.

In the uproar and confusion, one of the minions had no trouble in concealing his actions as he tipped the contents of the twist of parchment into a goblet and filled it with wine.

'Sire! Sire! Does my Lord need a drink?' Sir Bracy took the goblet from the minion who then melted away, disappearing in the growing crowd. Sir Osbert managed to gulp a mouthful, but it only served to make matters worse and he knocked the goblet from Sir Bracy's hand where it spilled over the stone floor, quickly disappearing between the cracks.

Sir Osbert was now in a delirium and close to death. His whole body went into wild convulsions and the crowd stood back in horrified fascination, in fear of what punishments would be meted out to pay for this murderous deed.

Sir Roland spoke to Sir Daltild: 'Sire, I fear he has been poisoned.'

'Never!' roared Sir Daltild. 'Never would I poison my honoured guest!'

Sir Osbert's breathing had become so laboured that all knew the end was nigh. By now most of the castle had been roused with the commotion and even the hunters and other servants poured into the Great Hall to watch the macabre spectacle. Albrus heaved a sigh of relief that his plot with Min had been fulfilled and Lady Mellissa had been freed from her betrothal. And as Sir Osbert's final breath left his body and winged its way to its destination, Albrus put his hands together in thanks. Dare he hope…? Perhaps in time…? Could there be a chance that the lovely Lady Melissa might…?

But as he prayed, the fair lady swooned, again, straight into the strong arms of Sir Roland, who scooped her up as if she were but a feather and carried her to a private chamber, where he laid her gently on golden draperies.

Meantime, Sir Daltild stamped his feet and wrung his hands in shame and despair. 'The Chef!' he boomed, 'Bring me The Chef! He must die for this monstrous deed!' Twenty or thirty of his strongest guards dashed from the Great Hall to do their lord's bidding. The minions had been right; it took nearly thirty men to seize The Chef, carry him to the battlements and hurl him down to the jagged rocks below, as he had done to so many others in his time.

Lord Osbert's men were appeased at this swift dispensation of justice, and none so much as Sir Roland. When the fair Mellissa opened her beautiful blue eyes to find Sir Roland stroking her raven's-wing hair and gazing at her tenderly, her heart went out to him, and his to her. So, before the party of guests left Castle Grimwall, there was another betrothal, with both the bride and groom happy and smiling and Mellissa went with her new husband to live in the rich and fertile lands beyond the sea.

Albrus nursed his broken heart, its mending swiftly aided by young Lettice who took full advantage of his sadness to comfort him. And by the time the hunters next ventured out into the forest they were accompanied by a pack of hounds who – after the sumptuous feast of a very large Chef – were as sleek and plump as anyone could ever wish for.

STORIES

PRECIOUS MORE THAN RUBIES.

JUDITH BARRIE

She found the diamond bracelet in the back of the carriage, just where she had left it, and heaved a sigh of relief. She had tucked it behind the cushion and now, in the general commotion and hubbub as the passengers settled back into their seats, she quickly palmed the bracelet and slipped it back in her pocket before she attended to the Lady Elizabeth's many needs.

The attack by the highwaymen had been swift and silent. They had emerged from the cover of a small copse of trees to the side of the deserted road, unnoticed by the dozing coachman until the leader had charged over, brandished a flintlock pistol at his head and shouted: 'Stand and deliver!' The coachman brought his horses to a standstill with a vicious tug of the reins while the four men jumped from their horses and threw open the carriage door.

'Out! All of you, out!'

The motley group of passengers were terrified, especially the ladies of the party. Lady Elizabeth uttered a mewling scream and clutched her hand to the glittering diamond and emerald ensemble that encircled her lily-white neck. Her maid, Agnes, sat stunned with eyes as round as saucers, afraid for her life and, realising that the robbers would quickly find the diamond and ruby bracelet in her pocket, swiftly stuffed it behind the cushion at the back of the seat.

In truth, she doubted that she would ever see it again, but stumbled out of the coach with the rest of the passengers and stood shivering in the lane, partly from the chilly October air, but mostly from fear for her life, or worse.

The leader, an over-grown man with cropped black hair and piercing dark eyes glittering behind a black mask, beckoned the ill-assorted group into the field at the side of the road. He pointed the pistol at them said menacingly: 'Hand over your valuables to my men, all of them, or I will not hesitate to kill you!' At this, the Lady Elizabeth swooned, and supported by Agnes and a gentleman, was conveyed to the side of the road, where she was seated on a large flat stone.

The three men quickly went round the group with a canvas bag, most of the party willingly handing over their precious items while the leader stood vigilant with the pistol. 'Everything!' he shouted, 'I want everything!'

'You must give him the necklace, m'lady,' whispered Agnes.

'No, I cannot!' she replied in anguish.

'Take it from her!' the man with the pistol instructed Agnes and she unfastened the clasp at the back. The man fairly tore it away from her hands, dropping it carelessly into the bag with the rest of the loot.

'Rings!' the leader shouted, and rings were swiftly collected.

A rather stout, elderly man was struggling to remove the fine set of rings from his chubby fingers. 'I cannot take them off,' he said, demonstrating the difficulty.

'Well, sir, we'll remove your fingers with them!' shouted the leader. A long knife was brandished by one of his colleagues and a renewed effort on behalf of the man rapidly achieved the required result.

When the robbers considered their collection completed, the leader motioned the passengers back into the coach. 'Not you,' he said to Lady Elizabeth, 'You look to have a lot more precious things about your person.' He handed the pistol to one of his men and seized the lady by the lace flounces at the top of her bodice.

'Please sir,' begged Agnes, 'please let her be! My lady is with child!' Agnes knew not whether that was the truth, but the robber looked long into Elizabeth's terrified eyes and threw her roughly aside, tearing her bodice as he did so. She stumbled back into the carriage with Agnes swiftly following her. He did not even bother to question Agnes, a lowly maid servant, in her plain grey muslin dress, not even a pendant in her ear.

The men leapt on their horses, the leader swept off his hat in a mock gesture, waved it in the air and shouted, 'I am much obliged to you and wish you all a speedy journey!' Then they departed as swiftly as they had come. The coachman climbed into his seat, still shaking, and sat stunned, as agitated as his horses.

STORIES

'Outrageous! The insolence of the wretch!' exclaimed the stout gentleman, finding himself lighter of a fine gold pocket watch and chain, along with four richly bejewelled rings, a gold cravat pin and the silver buckles from his shoes. His waistcoat hung limply about his person, the enamelled buttons having been removed.

The two nuns huddled back into their corner having lost no more than their silver crucifixes and amber rosary beads, for which they appeared to be offering grateful thanks to the Lord. The quiet couple seated next to Lady Elizabeth sat huddled together, the lady deprived of her wedding band and a fine garnet brooch, her husband of his silver pocket watch. 'The Gregory Gang, no doubt,' said her husband to the coach in general. 'I never thought I would live to see the day…'

The coach took off with a crack of the whip and a jolt and they travelled on their way in the gathering October gloom. 'We'll reach The Saracen's Head before dark, my lady,' said Agnes trying, without success, to comfort her weeping mistress, who seemed for once oblivious to her disordered coiffeur and the swell of her exposed bosom where her pink silk dress was torn.

There was a general stunned silence throughout the carriage, with the exception of the portly gentleman, who had become very red in the face and announced to all that his employers, Hoare and Co., bankers in London, would have much to say about such dastardly deeds.

'Scoundrels, the lot of 'em! They should be hung, drawn and quartered at the very least!'

Agnes settled quietly by her mistress, patting her hand from time to time in some effort to comfort her. She was fond of Lady Elizabeth in her own way and felt some pity towards her. After all, it had been Elizabeth's husband who had mistreated his wife so badly, who had dallied with Agnes until she had surrendered to his winning ways and now it was she, Agnes, who was with child; a bastard child who would never know his father.

'But do you really have love for me, Sire?' Agnes had asked of him. And he had replied that he had much love for her and would always care for her; he had sworn on his mother's grave; but then, he swore on just about anything that took his fancy. When she had told him that she was with child, he had promised to look after her, that she would want for nothing and the child would be raised as his own. But two days after her revelation, Agnes had been informed that Sir Marcus had been called away on urgent business to his properties in France, thence onward to Bohemia, and might not be back for many months.

Until now, she had been able to conceal her condition, but she knew that as the months went by, it would become plain and she would lose her position, disgraced and thrown out onto the streets to starve, a ruined woman.

It was then that she had hatched a plan. She had first come into the service of Sir Marcus and Lady Finch-Hatton when they had been staying at their London property, Hartington House, on Pall Mall. She had lived in London with her mother and siblings and considered herself fortunate indeed to have gained such a prestigious position as lady's maid on an annual income of nine pounds and ten shilling a year. As the springtime came, the family had gone up to Chatsmere House in Derbyshire, to spend the summer there, and now they were travelling back to the city for the winter season. Agnes decided that when they arrived back in London, she would take leave of the family, return to her mother's house and throw herself on her mercy, although, God knew, her mother had enough mouths to feed already.

Lady Elizabeth had a great quantity of fine jewellery to her name, most of which it seemed she seldom wore and didn't give a care to. Sure, the diamond and emerald necklace so recently purloined had been one of the finest pieces, recently given by Sir Marcus, but there was so much more… Surely, she would never miss a small piece, a brooch or a bracelet, something scarcely ever even noticed? Agnes espied a bracelet, long forgotten and tossed in an old casket amongst a jumble of pearls, sapphires, garnets, gold and silver. She had pulled it out when cleaning her Lady's bedchamber: it was purest gold setting with heart shaped links picked out in brilliant-cut diamonds. The centrepiece was a medallion of diamonds surrounding a large cabochon-cut ruby of the darkest blood red. The small clasp of gold had become a little tiresome and not worth the Lady's bother of wearing it.

STORIES

It had been an easy matter of slipping the bracelet into her pocket as she was packing a selection of gems for the journey to Hartington House. By the time the bracelet was missed when the family returned in the spring, she would have long disappeared into the teeming streets of the city, lost for ever.

After an unconscionable time John Higgs, the coachman, called down to the weary travellers that they had finally reached The Saracen's Head where they were to take refreshment and rest for the night. The inn was soon a-buzz with talk of the highway robbery, and it seemed that it had, indeed, been the notorious Gregory Gang who had terrorised the innocent coach party, as the banker had thought.

Lady Elizabeth was quickly covered by a voluminous cloak, and conveyed upstairs to the best room in the inn while Agnes scurried round, fetching hot water, tending the lady's hair and unpacking fresh clothes. Lady Elizabeth tore off the tarnished pink silk dress and told Agnes to dispose of it. 'I never want to see it again!' she said, casting it to the dusty floor and stamping her tiny velvet shoe on it in a fit of pique.

'Yes, m'lady.'

And all the while the lady was cursing: 'Tarnation! That pack of filthy shabbaroons! That scurvy wretch! Damn his blood, if Sir Marcus had been there he would have smote the scoundrel to the ground, pistol or no pistol!'

Agnes readily agreed with everything her mistress said, then went downstairs to fetch up some refreshment for them both. The innkeeper had prepared a substantial meal of rabbit pie with a few herbs and a pitcher of their finest Burgundy wine, but it was ill-received by the lady.

'I am sick to look on it,' she said, pushing the rabbit pie around the plate Agnes had served her.

'A little wine then, m'lady…?'

But the wine was pushed away after a single sip. 'Take it away. I could not possibly… I am quite undone…'

Agnes took the offending tray back downstairs and asked the innkeeper's wife if she could take it into the kitchen to satisfy her own hunger, to which the woman readily agreed.

After a restless night the party set off at dawn with much trepidation and still thirty miles to travel to the capital. It was a sombre mood inside the carriage with little conversation and Agnes thought much to her future and the future of the little one in her belly. She would have to find a willing goldsmith to buy the gems, but London was awash with pawnbrokers and artisans; she should find no hindrance in exchanging the bracelet for enough money to secure her future awhile.

The coach lumbered along and shortly after noon the fug of the city came into sight. At least they had reached their destination without further mishap. There was much restlessness and fidgeting amongst the passengers, hot and not a little bothered after their ordeal, all eager to alight and be on their way. One by one, the passengers left the carriage for the noisy, crowded and stinking streets until it finally arrived at Hartington House, on Pall Mall.

The residence had tall leaded windows, bas-relief stonework and a magnificent, hooded doorway, the architrave elaborately carved with scrolls of acanthus leaves. It was the most imposing house in a block of imposing houses. Lady Elizabeth was warmly received by the staff and soon found much comfort. The servants had lined the long marble hallway to greet them and Agnes thought wistfully that this might be the last time she would be welcomed into such a palatial dwelling. She had become accustomed to high-ceilinged rooms with exotic wallpaper covering the walls; the finest thick Persian carpets beneath her feet; a comfortable bed to lie on every night and, with Mrs Braddock in charge of the kitchens, never having to suffer an empty belly.

But no choice had been given to her. She knew now, without doubt, that Sir Marcus would deny any liaison with her and she would lose her position in an even worse plight. No, she must stay faithful to her plan.

The afternoon sun was sinking when Lady Elizabeth, still unable to take victuals, asked Agnes to prepare her a tisane of valerian to calm her fevered nerves, but when Agnes went down to the scullery, she found that there was no valerian to be had. 'Marie,' she asked of the parlour maid, 'Will you inform m'lady that I have just run out to the apothecary's to purchase some herbs?'

'Yes, miss,' was the sullen reply. Agnes hoped that the maid wouldn't notice the bulging bag she carried and question her, but Marie was not a bright girl and didn't appear to notice.

The reluctant parlour maid trudged upstairs on her errand and Agnes gathered her thick cloak around her, fingered the bracelet in her pocket and slipped out through the front door without a backward glance, dashing off into the gloomy dusk. She was much afraid: fearful of the reception from her mother, fearful of being found out in her theft of the jewels and, more than anything, fearful for the future of her child. She ran like the wind, through the milling throng, jostled and pushed in a way that she had almost forgotten, back to her other life in London praying that she would be lost among the other seven hundred thousand souls sharing the city with her.

She pulled up the hood of her cloak and slowed her pace, partly because her breath had failed her and partly because she did not want to draw attention from prying eyes. But she walked briskly enough through the streets heading in a northward direction, past opticians and booksellers, clothiers and bird-sellers, buffeted by the stinking crowds. She thought on Lady Elizabeth and wondered how she would manage with only a housemaid to take down her hair and prepare her for bed. There would be more than valerian called for before the night was out.

Her bag became heavy and she thought on the tightly packed contents. She had managed to secure most of her precious wardrobe – it would be a long time before she would find fine linens again – and, rolled very small at the bottom, the discarded pink silk dress. Ten or twelve yards of fabric which had cost eighteen and sixpence a yard; a year's wages spent carelessly on a single garment. Now it would make many garments for herself and her sister Hannah.

By the time she reached the house where her mother lived on Appleby Street, almost within sight of the execution site at Tyburn Hill, Agnes was spattered with mud and slops, and on the verge of collapse. She found her mother in the same cramped house, sleeping in the old wooden chair before a few smouldering embers.

'Mother,' she whispered. 'Mother, it's me, Agnes. I've come home.'

Her mother slowly opened her eyes, looked long and hard at her daughter and, noticing the slight curve of her belly said, 'So! You've brought a child with you, I see!'

Agnes lied to her mother about the diamond bracelet. She told her about the 'courtship' by Sir Marcus, but that when he found she was expecting his child, as he was unable to wed her, he gave her the jewels to take care of them both as the child grew. There was a lot of truth in the story she told, but an even greater quantity of wishful thinking. But her mother accepted the tale and after a few days, Agnes had told the tale so many times that she started to believe it herself.

Her mother, Peggy, made her living as a washerwoman and Agnes, despite her condition, was put to help, carrying pails of water from the standpipe down the street, heating it on the fire. Her sister, Hannah, was now fourteen and working as a needlewoman with a tailor on Tottenham Court Road and earning a shilling a week, which paid half the rent. Her brother, Thomas, had been working at Billingsgate market for two years and was earning nearly ten shillings a week. His mother was grateful for a few shillings from him and for the left-over mackerel and the odd dab of meat that he brought home from the market nearly every day but fearful that at nineteen, he would soon want to marry and leave to make a home of his own.

Agnes shared a bed with Thomas, staying up to doze by the fire until Thomas left for work just after two in the morning in order to get to the market in time for the mackerel boats to arrive. The warmth of the bed became a luxury she relished, and Hannah would often waken and creep in beside her, snuggling beside her swelling belly. Their young brother, John, had been taken from them of a fever a few months before and their father, Joseph had died many years before in an accident, falling from the roof of a nearby house, where he was fixing tiles.

STORIES

Sometimes Agnes sat and wept at the plight of her family, cold and miserable and hungry most of the time; then she thought of Sir Marcus traipsing round the continent, supping and dicing and not a care in the world. Certainly no thought to the babe he had left behind.

And all the time, a diamond and ruby bracelet lay snug in her pocket, but it became ever more urgent that the diamonds must be converted into cash. This proved a much greater task than Agnes had ever imagined.

At that time, London was awash with all manner of in-comers – Irish, blacks, Jews, gypsies and Huguenots. Along with the new coffee-houses, there was a pawnshop on every corner, but her first reception there was a harsh one. The old man was as bent and twisted and gnarled as an ancient tree. She placed the bracelet on the counter before him and he looked at it with astonishment.

'Where did you get this from?' he demanded harshly.

'Sir, it was given to me...'

'Take it away! Take it out of my shop at once before I fetch the constable! I don't want to end up in the Old Bailey and carted up that Hill to be hanged,' he said ominously, his eyes turning in the direction of Tyburn. Agnes hurriedly put the bracelet back in her pocket and scurried back into the street, her heart beating fit to burst.

She thought again about Lady Elizabeth and the way she had carelessly tossed her jewels aside as if they were worthless trinkets. The way she would have Agnes stand behind her to secure a pearl necklace only to change her mind and demand the diamonds in its stead, then change her mind back to the pearls, stamping her little velvet slippers in frustration as if it were the necklace's fault that she was displeased. The bracelet must be got rid of before it was missed, but not at the price of her neck on Tyburn.

Fear prevented her from taking it elsewhere for several weeks until the need for money drove her to seek the services of a Huguenot artisan she had heard tell of, named Joseph de Batz. His shop was deep in the city, in a maze of huddled dwellings, far from where she lived with her mother. It was now a snowy January day and almost time for the child to be born. She timidly opened the door of the otherwise empty shop and walked inside, quiet as a mouse. It appeared that there was a short man behind the counter, but he was seated in a chair and when he stood, he towered above her, causing her great alarm.

'Sir...' she stuttered. Her mouth became dry and she felt a little faint as the babe started to kick at her. Her distress was obvious to him as he marked her advanced condition.

'Can I get you some water, my dear?' He did not wait for an answer, but disappeared behind the curtain at the back of the shop and brought back a cup of water and a wooden stool for her to sit on. His kindness touched her greatly and she began to weep.

'What is it that I can do for you?' he asked gently.

'Sir...' She paused, looking into his fine blue eyes, his fair hair and brows. He produced a linen handkerchief for her to dab her cheek and waited patiently.

'Sir... You cannot help but be aware of my condition. The father of my child is a fine gentleman, rich and powerful. And I was a humble serving maid to his wife. When this... happened, I had to leave his employ and he gave to me a piece of jewellery, to give...'

'Yes, yes. I understand,' he said softly, sparing her any further embarrassment. 'Let me see the piece.'

Agnes drew out the bracelet and placed it on the counter before him.

'My, my!' he said in astonishment. 'That is a splendid piece, my dear. The gentleman must have cared for you very much!' He went back behind the counter and drew out from a drawer a much-used eyeglass which he placed in his right eye.

'My, my! I have never in my life had sight of such a ruby!' He took up a quill in his right hand and started to write down notes. 'Ceylon, undoubtedly! Cabochon-cut, a stone so fine, it might have been used at some time for a regal... Do you know where the stones were from originally?'

'No, sir. It was a gift, I did not question...'

'No. No, of course not.' He changed the eyeglass to his left eye and Agnes watched, fascinated as he changed the quill to his left hand and continued to write his notes.

'The ruby alone is worth... well, a fortune, my dear. And such fine diamonds. Brilliant-cut! There must... be well-nigh... a hundred of them all told! And all of a good size!' It was difficult to tell who was the more astonished, Joseph de Batz or Agnes. He changed the eyeglass, and quill, back to his right side and made further notes. 'Yes, my dear, he must have been *very* fond of you to give you such a...'

He repeated his performance with the eyeglass and the quill, much to Agnes's great amusement, and for the first time in a very long while her tears turned to smiles. 'Well,' he said finally. 'I cannot buy the bracelet from you in its entirety – the ruby alone must be worth a thousand pounds! I do not have so much money available to me, but perhaps only one stone at a time... it would be a great shame to break it, but...'

'A thousand pounds...' she murmured uncomprehending.

He noticed what lovely eyes she had, how the smile lit up her beautiful face. And her heart skipped a beat – she had never met such a fine gentleman.

'Perhaps... Perhaps, we could come to some mutually satisfactory arrangement...' he said, hopefully.

And come to an arrangement they did. Joseph de Batz proved to be a much more devoted lover than Sir Marcus Finch-Hatton had been. They were wed in the springtime, with Agnes's baby daughter – named Elizabeth as Agnes had always admired the name – in attendance wearing an exquisite miniature pink silk dress embroidered by her Aunt Hannah. And as the happy years went by, Agnes had much to thank her dear husband for and the way he wrote with both hands.

A CAT'S NINE LIVES

Rosemary Swift

The theory that a cat has many lives varies from culture to culture. The most commonly accepted is "A cat has nine lives. For three he plays, for three he strays and for the last three he stays."

It so happened that my first existence was in Egypt and almost perfect ('purrfect' in my tongue) because I was much pampered by a Pharaoh, which did me no favours upon his sudden death because as they mummified him they also mummified me! The idea was I was to accompany him to the afterlife where we would live in harmony alongside others who had joined him on his last journey.

Suddenly, I am a mewing creature again looking for the teat. Alas, the litter had been plucked from our dam and thrust into a sack, which was filling with water. I am aware of a child wailing and of the string round the neck of the bag being loosened and me being lifted out. My siblings were not so lucky and drowned down a well. It turns out I had been rescued by little Tommy Stout who I lived beside for many happy years, killing the mice in his father's barn.

It is me who now has teats upon re-birth. Having many litters courtesy of feral visitors, I lived with an old lady in the woods who gathered medicinal herbs. Her neighbours were grateful to take advantage of her potions until the shadow of witchcraft covered the land. I sent my latest litter scattering when they came for the old lady but I was at her side even when they burned her at the stake. I wish to gloss over such a death but I am glad I stayed in the arms of my beloved human and gave her comfort.

I had a happier existence next time around bobbing along on the high seas despite suffering injuries. The main one being the loss of an eye as had my master, who now lay dying on the deck of the HMS Victory. Horatio used to whisper to me that we managed better with one eye each than anybody else on board with their full complement of optic means. His body was sent back to England for a state funeral but I did not accompany it. Heartbroken, I had crawled into one of the cannons where I was accidentally ramrodded and fired out in a hundred pieces.

STORIES

With large rounded eyes and no tails, the Manx cat is distinctive to the isle of the same name. Viking raiders thought the tails of these cats to be a lucky charm so according to folklore, mother cats took to biting off the tails of their litters to avoid the kittens being manhandled by ruffians. Known as Rumpy Stubbin (nicknames used by the islanders for our breed of cat) and being social, tame and active by nature, I was highly prized as a rodent catcher. Sadly, a common deformity of the Manx cat is to suffer from spinal abnormalities, affecting the central nervous system and this was to be my fate. It was one of the few times that I died from natural causes; being given a cosy bed near the open roaring fire I was much lamented as I drifted away.

Several dogs and pigeons have won the Dickin Medal since it was first awarded in 1943 but only one cat. I too had my moment when known as Sevastopol Tom; during a certain siege of the Crimean War, I led starving British and French soldiers to a secret cache of food. I was brought back as a pet to England. Upon my death by natural causes, I was stuffed and displayed but this makes me feel uncomfortable, reminding me of my first earthly life.

Gifted from his Secretary of State, Abraham Lincoln was the first President to have cats residing in the White House. Lincoln used a gold fork with which to feed his beloved Tabby at White House dinners and claimed his other cat Dixie was smarter than his whole cabinet. I was a later edition to the household being one of three motherless kittens, Lincoln rescued whilst visiting General Grant during the Civil War. He regularly played with us kittens to relieve stress. There was much meowing when Lincoln did not come home one night. Soon afterwards, whilst playing around the feet of the many horses in the Mews, I was fatally crushed by a carriage wheel.

One of my favourite incarnations was as the pet of a local thespian, with a particular love of appearing in pantomimes in the village hall. I was that devoted to him, he knew I would behave alongside him on stage when he appeared as Dick Whittington. This took away an acting part from a small child but my owner loved the authenticity of it and so did the audience. However, this took a turn when a vindictive youth lowered a sandbag from the stage rafters crushing me flat. As I drifted out of consciousness, I could hear my master bellowing with grief.

Now up to date with my reminiscences, my present reincarnation will definitely be my last earthly one but who knows how the 9-lives theory will pan out in outer space because I am strapped in the cockpit of a spacecraft awaiting blast-off at the side of my owner who is vacating Planet Earth to retire to a space station. A Boston Animal Behavioural Clinic has declared that cats are intelligent enough to have their own thoughts as structurally the feline brain and the human brain are very similar. A dog will always work alongside a human but perhaps a cat in the cosmos will truly be able to surpass – and dictate to – a human.

STORIES
MAYDAY... MAYDAY

ROSEMARY SWIFT

The flare had gone up and now Paul – in a leaking boat with his elderly Dad, Tommy – was waiting for help to arrive from the nearby shore. Paul felt embarrassed about not checking the boat more thoroughly, having been carried away with the emotions attached to its usage; one aspect of the trip, on this May Bank Holiday was the hope that Tommy would be stimulated and recall his Merchant Navy days, having served many years at sea whilst Paul and his brothers Andrew and James had been at home with Mum, Nancy. Although Tommy interacted with his boys when on leave, it was Nancy who had kept the family ticking over, even fitting in a part-time job at the local Bookies.

Paul recalled the day his Mum had asked somebody to place a bet for her (not being allowed to do so herself) and Marine Boy had romped home 100 to 1. Somehow she had scraped together a fiver to place for a win. He turned to his Dad with a smile and repeated this memory out loud... in fact, very loud, his Dad being extremely deaf these days. Although his Dad returned the smile, he looked bewildered. It was just so sad for Tommy to be suffering from Alzheimer's in his later years, not helped by the recent death of Nancy, his lovely bride of over 50 years. The main reason father and son were out to sea on this lovely sunny late spring day was to scatter her ashes; Paul carrying out the task as his brothers lived some distances away.

A boat could have been chartered with a skipper on board from a specialist firm but Paul thought it a good idea to use the family boat. Unfortunately, its upkeep had been neglected for a number of years – in fact, from the onslaught of his Dad's condition – and by now the feet of Paul and his Dad were quite soggy. Tommy had seemed to recognise what they had done when tipping up the urn and had dispersed petals on the ashes floating in the water, his eyes dimming with tears. He had sniffed the fragrant yellow roses but had not been aware that these were the symbol of a Golden Wedding anniversary. Paul's wife Sue had thoughtfully ordered them from a local florist shop, aptly named Aqua Lily, it being on the High Street of a seaside town.

A generous donation had been made to the town's Lifeboat Society following Nancy's death and now her widower and a son were to take advantage of its excellent service. Tommy, upon his retirement had not joined the volunteers going out to sea but he had assisted in many other ways so when rescue came he would be known to whatever crew was on standby but it would be doubtful if Tommy would know them. It had been most upsetting at Nancy's recent funeral when Tommy, looking baffled, had said to his youngest son: "I know your name is James but who are you?" and he had stared right past his eldest son Andrew. Both brothers, although having been kept in the loop by Paul, had not realised to what extent their father had deteriorated and a plan of action for specialised future care was now in the pipeline.

By now, Paul could see a RNLI boat speeding through the water. As he turned to ensure his Dad was safe and ready to be transferred, Paul missed his footing and tumbled backwards into the sea. As he splashed and spluttered he was relieved that the lifeboat was now pulling alongside but he was more distracted by the fact that his father was stood up in the damaged boat and Paul and RNLI crew alike were amazed to hear Tommy clearly giving out orders: "Man overboard, crew stand by for action, throw a lifebuoy, lift him aboard, turn him on his front, ensure no water in his lungs, cover him with a rug, give him an issue of rum."

Sat side by side as they reached the shore, Tommy seemed to have returned to a state of lethargy but Paul felt his left hand being squeezed very tightly and knew that, once again in his life, Dad had looked out for him.

STORIES
VIOLET THE SHRINK
ROSEMARY SWIFT

Violet, a psychoanalyst, was used to dealing with disturbed 'clients', a word she preferred to 'patients' as she had no patience. In fact, it was a case of the biblical "Physician, heal thyself". Her own upbringing was what led her to becoming a shrink – not so much out of empathy but more a case of understanding what was required in the job, being brought up neglected by hippy-parents who had, as was locally remembered, dabbled. Violet's cold personality did not lead to a large client base so, although she yearned to be rich and independent, she still relied on the munificence of her widowed mother by them living together in the family home.

Everything was bearable whilst her mother was still active; cooking meals on the Aga, using ingredients from their own sprawling garden planted by Violet's father, now deceased. However, Violet was put out when her mother was diagnosed with advanced glaucoma; symptoms having been ignored for a long time by using plant-like substances as an attempted cure of which Eye Specialists were made aware. Violet was not after becoming a carer rather than being cared for. One of her patients had decided to cease his long-term habit of using LSD and similar substances and there had been such an improvement he no longer needed Violet's services. At his last session, he had dumped a carrier bag at her feet. It was upon examination of the bag's contents that gave her the idea.

After using a computer at an out-of town library (so as not to be traced to her office or home equipment) Violet had read up about how the pupils of the eyes could be dilated by the sap of datura suaveolens, more commonly known as Angel's Trumpet. After looking up a picture of this plant, she was quietly excited as she thought there was some in the large sprawling garden behind her mother's mansion of a house. It was built so long ago, that it was also home to many creatures – in fact rat traps had recently been laid in the kitchen, her mother being frantic at the thought of any gaining access to the many other rooms. One such room was designated as a work studio for Violet's hobby of sewing, where costumes were created for Church events. "Oh, what would we do without you,

Violet," the Parish Committee regularly gushed, making her feel special – something her parents had never done. She had come across an old fur coat purchased many moons ago at a Church Bazaar and which would come in handy for a costume for the coming production of 'Dick Whittington' and it had now been transformed into that of a King Rat.

At this very moment, she was putting drops in her mother's eyes. Stop wriggling, you old bat was what she thought but what she said was: "Oh, mother, you know you need your medication." "But just lately, they have been smarting too much – I am sure you are overdosing" her mother complained. Violet retorted: "Well, how can I when you just have a regular monthly prescription?" But what she had been doing was adding to the prescription.

Violet next pandered to her mother by laying out afternoon tea on the patio with a vase of Angel's Trumpets as centrepiece on the table. She carefully added LSD to her mother's cup of lemon tea and laid out the sandwiches and cakes. After partaking of the meal, her mother became extremely agitated so Violet offered to go for any appropriate medication. She re-appeared wearing the King Rat costume, upon sight of which her mother – whose eyes were already dilated – jumped up screaming and backed away, sending her tumbling down the steep stone steps on to the lawn. Satisfied her mother lay dead, Violet rubbed some of the Angel's Trumpets onto her mother's hands and then raised her mother's cold fingers so as to rub them into her mother's staring eyes.

When an ambulance arrived, Violet – having washed her own hands thoroughly and changed back into normal clothes – appeared to show appropriate grief but her mind was racing with the thought of selling up the home, moving into a trendy apartment in the local town and enjoying a comfortable life from inheritance monies.

STORIES
GERALD'S DREAM
Catherine Grant-Salmon

Gerald, the farmer sat in his armchair after an enjoyable day out at the Annual County Agricultural Show. His prize bull, Rambo had come third for his breed in the show, quite an accolade for a small farm. Rambo is a Black Hereford hulking beautiful great beast with flaring nostrils and mighty thighs from excellent pedigree stock. Gerald would be tempted with offers from envious farmers to sell his prize asset for a considerable sum of money to improve their own herds or keeping Rambo to have a lot of fun in a field full of heifers. These were options to ponder or sell his semen, the bull's, not Gerald's. Artificial insemination without romance and sex. This was not the desired outcome for Rambo who wanted to fumble and frolic in the fields giving frisky ladies a good time. He wanted his oats and barley. Instead of delivering his precious semen in a dish to an unsympathetic vet.

That could all wait, as tonight Gerald was more than content to relax with a glass of rum to toast his good fortune. Betty, his granddaughter had been so excited to go to the show. She had decided to be a farmer or show jumper when she grew up. Gerald smiled as it was only last week that she had wanted to be an astronaut, vet or train driver. Nothing was beyond bounds to an innocent child with a lifetime ahead. He thought about what it would be like to be young again. When you could imagine being the cartoon character 'Mr Benn, from Watch with Mother' walking into a fancy dress shop to be greeted by a mysterious exotic man wearing a fez. The shop owner directing Mr Benn into a changing room to metamorphosise into a different character. There he would enter another door leading into a world of adventure and fantasy. Gerald always liked it when 'Mr Benn' was transformed into the fireman and orchestra conductor best. He hated clowns that made him frown. There were never any soul destroying dreary tedious jobs and mundane existence in the world of 'Mr Benn'. He was not clock watching until it was time to go home.

Gerald was thankful for his life, doing a job that he loved. Farming was a vocation not a chore. He didn't mind getting up at all hours to tend his flock, and growing crops on his small holding in the countryside. There was never a time when he was tired of the landscape. Mother nature conjured autumnal hues and snowcapped frosty winters; with vibrant lush springs and sun parched golden summers.

As he drifted off to sleep nice and snug in his favourite armchair. There beside him was Judd, his cocker spaniel lying on the hearth rug. Suddenly, he was hearing claxon horns, whistles, and bells. Shrieking children cheering and laughing at him. Then, much to his surprise, a custard hit him in the face. Followed by an enormous water pistol squirting him on the bum. All the children laughed and jeered. Thinking it hilariously funny. The torment continued as he tripped over a box full of balloons and smelly socks.

"What on earth is this hell and where am I?" he yelled over the hubbub of noise from the audience.

"You are in the circus, my friend" said the ringmaster "There are trapeze artists, acrobats and dancing horses... watch out you are going to get knocked down by Zimbo, one of the other clowns."

Much to poor Gerald's consternation, he was now wearing a bright orange curly wig and enormous purple shoes, complete with a big red nose and painted on white silly smile. He wanted to run a mile and wondered what to do as trumpets blasted out. There was nowhere for him to escape. The commotion carried on as plates were smashed and luminous green foam congealed on the floor. Then he noticed a Wendy House in the far corner and popped inside. Only to be strangled with a string of sausages. The audience was in hysterics and cheered, egging on for more. Poor Gerald feared wondering what on earth to do now.

"Jump over there" he heard someone shout, and the next moment had fallen down his cellar after hitting his head on a bookcase.

What was going on? He was now at market selling Rambo for a princely sum of a few beans. That'll be no use unless there's a golden egg at the top of the beanstalk. My name's not Jack and I will be given the sack. Gerald admitting he was also scared of heights. The agony continued as he tried clambering on slippery vines and slid straight down, falling into a crumpled heap. It was a game of snakes and ladders or Kerplunk that sunk. Who gives a Buckeroo?

STORIES

Woosh suddenly, he was in Venice. The city of love and romance. Mills and Boon fat chance more of a mystery in his book. Gerald was now being chased by a llama, duck, and Wolfhound. They chased him through the back streets, palazzos, and cafes. Then he managed to hide in a shop for a minute or two before he felt the llamas spit on the back of his neck. Passersby were transfixed by such an extraordinary sight and started taking photos. Thinking they were one of the comedy acts embarking from a cruise ship blighting the landscape. The llama was now too starstruck to give a second thought to his prey.

"Please help me" Gerald begged, and nobody took a blind bit of notice.

His heart was pounding and he managed to swerve away from the crowds. Knocking over boxes of fruit and vegetables. Things couldn't get any worse, surely. Then he slipped on a banana skin and splattered ricotta. Out of the corner of his eye, he spotted a giant Gorgonzola menacingly rolling into his way. This was the big Cheese, otherwise known as 'boss.' All poor Gerald could do was mumble and try to run. The sound of church bells rang out and an ice cream van played the theme tune to The Magic Roundabout.

"Hi Dude, what's happening man?" said the laidback giant rabbit standing beside a tangerine and purple coloured tree. Dylan had magically appeared holding to a signpost to the magnificent Rialto Bridge.

Zebedee was springing about, reminding Florence it was time for bed. Brian the snail went into this shell. Ermentrude, the cow was hoping to be on Rambo's hit list. Gerald had to find a way out of his hallucinogenic trip. He would never look at a bowl of pasta again and stick to a tin of spaghetti hoops for his tea. On hindsight, those mushrooms eaten in his carbonara tasted funny. An over ambitious culinary experiment bought from the market. They were a load of Shiitake.

Gerald decided to mingle with all the tourists in a crowd and plan how to make his escape from Venice. An innocuous yacht called the Mia Rosa moored on the edges of the quayside caught his eye. He noticed there appeared to be no one around and was a great opportunity to flee. Tentatively jumping on board, convinced that he was being chased by the llama, duck, wolfhound and boss. Surprizingly the yacht was easy to manoeuvre. What a song and dance. This sailing lark is a doddle and he relaxed, enjoying the sun glistening on calm waves as land was becoming a distant and faded landscape. Cruise ships statuesquely moored were reduced to model boats. Gerald started to quite like the idea of being a castaway with no pressures in life. The thought of sailing to far horizons and new adventures. Coral reefs and crustaceans; mermaids and marlins.

What was that noise he suddenly heard? A menacing growl from the lower deck. Just a figment of his vivid imagination or not. There was no one in sight except for a withering looking spider. Should Gerald scarper or swim? The animal growled again and paced the deck. Gerald gingerly tiptoed over to the entrance to look at his fellow castaway. He was unable to work out if the tattered animal was a dog or wolf. Then the animal began wailing much to Gerald's consternation. Menacingly gnashing its teeth and climbing the stairs to welcome him onboard. It was a wolf and, feeling frantic, he threw a cake to bide some time.

Gerald heard a gunshot and, before his very eyes, a buxom pneumatic blond in a skimpy bikini and mink coat appeared. She was dripping in diamonds and blew out the smoke. Licking her lips and approached him whilst gently stroking her throbbing pistol. The stranger spoke in a Russian accent.

"Good evening, I have been expecting you and what have you brought my sweet?"

Gerald had nothing to offer. He rummaged in his pockets and found a golden red crispy apple. A menace shoplifting in Venice. He gave it to the mysterious woman. Without saying a word. All was quiet at sea except for the splash of an octopus and basking shark. She ravenously bit into the apple and licked her lips. Gerald was transfixed by her curvaceous hips and juice trickling down her ample cleavage. She was a golden delicious pink lady from Bramley with russet tones. He felt himself crumble before her very eyes. Her hideous cackling laugh erupted the solicitous sexual silence. She was turning into a decrepit withered old hag, who he didn't want to shag. Granny Smith started stroking his arm and chest. Emitting a

STORIES

subtle growl from her jowls. Temptation and torment. Lust and longing.

There was a smell of burning - he was toast. Without a life vest, he hoped for the best as she clawed at his trembling body. Eager for a taste of his flesh and blood. Chewing on his bones and sunbathing on the deck, her hair was now grey tattered and torn. Transforming into a wolf. So much for dirty dreaming - it was all scheming. He yelled out and woke with a jolt. As he felt his flesh ripped open and body torn apart.

There beside him was Judd fast asleep and the carriage clock ticking. Not a wolf in sight. Just an empty glass on a side table with Betty's book of Fairytales. A bitten apple, wolf, and pistol on the cover of his thriller alongside. Gerald remembered eating gorgonzola and crackers for supper. Cheese always gave him nightmares.

He yawned and wiped sleep from his eyes. Dishevelled and stretched out. It was four in the morning and day was dawning. His beautiful Friesian girls with bulbous udders needed milking soon. He had pigs, sheep, and goats to feed. Harvesting his orchard filled with many varieties of apples. Sowing seeds and picking crops. Gerald decided that artificial insemination was not for him and sympathised with Rambo. His girls would love a bit of bully and deliver a considerable sum of money for their offspring. Rambo deserved his wicked way in the hay. This was all a labour of love.

MASQUERADE

CATHERINE GRANT-SALMON

Writing Challenge:
The Quality Street Gang

Flaky McGoldrick and Cokey Nolan were members of the Quality Street Gang. The gang operated in Manchester from the nineteen sixties to eighties. They were an infamous and notorious group of vagabonds, describing themselves as a 'social friendship between a group of men'. They had been brought up in working class socially deprived towns of Harpurhey, Collyhurst and Ancoats to name a few.

Each member was named after a chocolate nicknamed from the Quality Street advert. Flaky took on the moniker of the green foil triangle, attributed to the three sides to his personality. Honest, Hard and Hilarious. Cokey was the purple one, covered in bruises due to forever getting in fights and carrying heavy bags of coal. He was a hidden tough nut encased in a soft caramel exterior and chocolate shell. The lad had done well and could make life hell. Inside their smart suits, shirts, coats, and ties, secrets and lies of their nicknames were discretely hidden and forbidden. Flaky had an emerald, triangle pin badge in his suit jacket inside pocket lining and purple amethyst stud was sewn behind Cokey's favourite tie. They were both married to local lasses, Marilyn aka Strawberry Delight due to her strawberry blond hair and Coconut Éclair was an exotic taste of paradise: Juanita, childhood name Joan, always dressed in blue. Her art of sultry seduction was to devour a Cadbury's flake in an overflowing porcelain bath full of bubbles, licking her lips and purring with delight. Thankfully there was a black market in stolen coal from the purple one, otherwise the emersion heater would never have been switched off and their ceilings always looked a sight. Twin brothers Anthracite and Nutty Slack were part of the smuggling coal racket. Cokey had bludgeoned one of a rival gang members with an iron coal skuttle and used a brass fireside companion set to sweep up the mess.

The two couples were childhood sweethearts and lived in the picturesque village of Roe Green. They drank at the Cock pub and

STORIES

dined at the Ellesmere with duck a l'orange a favourite, and crepe suzette for dessert. Behind the chintz curtains and dinner parties, secrets lurked. The Quality Street Gang were never seen and heard, but what really did go on in nineteen sixties one bus village, Roe Green? Was the Quality Street Gang masquerading on secret missions?

Cokey and Flaky were respectable members of the Independent Methodist Church congregation on the Green. Always happy helping at Jumble Sales, village fetes and took pride in joining the mass church walk around the village in summer. Brass bands, brownies, guides, scouts and cubs. Over sixties, infant Sunday school and youth clubs. They were all part of the vibrant village church hub. What most of the congregation and church elders were not privy and oblivious to see were the dubious notes left strategically in certain hymn and prayer books handed out by the sainted two amongst new worshippers invited to join the congregation. They seemed to have connections with other ministries and brought along guest preachers to talk about salvation and redemption or evils and sins of temptation. The hymn 'All things bright and beautiful' was sung with gusto as furtive whispers passed around the chosen few sitting in the same pews.

Their ladies took an interest in homely matters frequenting the wool shop and buying knitting patterns for balaclavas and thick black wool, on the premise of giving comfort and warmth to destitute orphans in far off distant foreign lands. They were passing on knitting needles and wool for instruments of torture, stabbing, tying up and gagging with pastel shades of baby two- and three-ply thread. Applique and crochet squares stuffed over mouths and blood-soaked wounds. Piercing and prodding with a crochet hook, only a contortionist and sadomasochist would enjoy.

The newsagent was not exempt from their subterfuge and queuing outside for a Saturday night Football Pink. Cokey and Flaky always giving one of their new invited friends a wink and praise George Best. Buying cigarettes, chewing gum and chocolate bars from vending machines. Reading the window display of postcard adverts. 'Mrs Bloggs from Lyon Street wanting a toilet seat' was a prime example. A debate about the state of Rhodesia, an article promising a new housing estate in Hulme and entertainment at Belle

Vue were interspersed with football reports, random crossword clues and car sales adverts. This made the Manchester Evening news and Football Pink an entertaining read. They were filled with spelling mistakes and printing errors, hidden clues to night terrors and heists. The Enigma machine had nothing on the expertise of the Quality Street Gang with secret codes and knuckle breakers.

Cokey would nip down to the ironmongers on Greenleach Lane to buy his paraffin, firelighters, and clothes pegs. Flaky chipped in with firewood, glue, screws, and nails. Were they really making coffins and performing cremations, or just good at DIY? Only one could surmise what they were doing at home.

The gang used to hide their bounty under the cogs of the number twelve bus and exchange messages at the Lancashire United Transport depot on Worsley Road, Swinton. There was always a ten-minute wait for a new driver and conductor, same on the East Lancs Road at the Ellesmere as a diversion on the thirty-one. Roe Green was embroiled in espionage and trouble, safe in a hidden bubble. The station signal box at Beesley Green Junction concealed parking fines and tickets, court orders and disguises. The gang could make a quick getaway along the railway lines and risk getting hit by a rare steam train out of sight. Furtive notes, weapons and packages were secreted in the outside toilets of nearby Roe Green Infants school with its grotesque green mouldy floor, Izal toilet paper, smelling of stale wee and distemper. The detritus of nervous and excitable children ingrained in permeated walls and doors. It would have put anyone off the scent of crime.

Were bodies and illegal pickings hidden inside the sidings of the old colliery railway line (Sandersons Sidings) that went through the woods from Astley pit or under the old St Marks school cellar? Did they take advantage to bury the loot in the soon to be demolished lodge on Greenleach Lane and rubble of houses on Hawthorne Drive? Making way for the new-fangled exciting M62 motorway that splintered Worsley woods into a dichotomy of two, destroying vegetation and wildlife. What lies hidden in the concrete foundations and aggregate tarmacadam of postmodernism Britain and lurking in shady wooded places? Do trees look like hidden faces

STORIES

and dismembered limbs? Be careful where you walk and listen to others talk.

Strawberry Delight, Cokey's wife, served behind a counter in the Post Office and loved getting her hands on the bacon slicer. Constructing a Lyons Maid square block ice cream and matching cone to a naughty excited child who'd just picked their nose was part of the job. She liked to hear the gossip of locals and made friends with customers, instantly knowing who had a Mothers Pride or Hovis. Cokey paid his bills to the postmaster behind the security grill buying postal orders, a stamp and loaf of bread. Nothing was said about the correspondents' dubious addresses on the other side of town, or airmails and packets to South America. Cokey carried cash in his pockets, pristine, suited and booted after showering from work. Amethysts were a sign to protect him from danger and clear his mind.

Occasionally the couples would go walking through Worsley woods, crossing over the canal bridge to the other side onto Barton Road. There they would meet one the gang members parked outside the Bridgewater pub, to be given a lift in his Ford Zephyr to the Clifton Grange Hotel in Whalley Range via the Eccles and Stretford by-pass. George Best, Mancunian dandies and landed gentry members of the establishment socialised at the watering hole, owned by Philomena Lynott.Cokey and Flaky would congregate with their mates founding members Jimmy 'the weed' Donnelly, Jim Swords, and his brother Joe. Bestie liked Caramel Swirl and was his kind of girl - psychedelic hotpants, white boots and model looks. Miss Wythenshawe nineteen sixty-seven, he was in heaven.

Their residence in Roe Green ended suddenly, a visiting church missionary was on a crusade. He had smelt something fishy, and collars were felt, prayers said and promises made. Cokey and Flaky, spouses and all moved to another unsuspecting quiet picturesque village hidden in the Greater Manchester conurbation.

Police Constable John Stalker was the undercover preacher. Life carried on in Roe Green as if nothing had happened. Or did it anyway, or were these words written by the vivid imagination of a curious child?

BAH HUMBUG

Catherine Grant-Salmon

Writing Challenge:
Halloween theme

Alan hated the commercialisation of Halloween and all its trappings. He was a traditionalist at heart, believing that pumpkins, witches, and black cats were the only things synonymous with Halloween. In his twilight years, widowed and lonely, attending church gave him social and spiritual support. This nonsense about trick or treat beggars belief, typical of American's hijacking religious and pagan customs. Pumpkins had been lit and carved out since pagan times to drive away evil spirits. Alan wished he could do the same with the pesky kids from across the road. He tried not to be a curmudgeonly wizened old man with creaky limbs and bent back.

The only exception to his profound dislike of Halloween was pumpkins, which he talked about at Pine Lodge Senior Citizens Centre. He liked to see them cut out and carved with a tea light embedded in the centre. How they brightened up the darkest of late October nights, keeping adults and children occupied scooping out the lush vibrant innards. The fun of carving out a grizzly face, quite like his own in the mirror. Small, plump, squidgy, large, two for three pounds at Morrisons and Tesco do their best. He had seen them on his trips to the shops.

"Advertisements for pumpkin picking and hog roast barbecues. Toffee apples and popcorn. Scary movie and Halloween pyjamas, whatever will they think of next." Alan remembered trips out with his late wife, Jean, to Southport, on their way stopping at a farm shop and admiring the Autumn fields filled with brightly coloured crops of marrows, squashes, and pumpkins. They contrasted to the faded days of grey and leafless skeletal trees. All grown in fertile rich, engorged, malted, brown soil. Birds hovering for debris and seeds. Geese, ducks, and streams of swallows migrating to warmer climates. Cabbages grown in strategic lines, an odd jolly scarecrow to brighten up the skyline. Lucious vibrant red berries and plump rose hips complementing frosty opaque cobwebs on hedgerows. Children and parents picking a pumpkin with zeal. Which one

STORIES

should they choose or propose? Touch and prod, give it a nod. An iconic objectification and glorification of orangeness, bold, tough, and smooth, an enticement.

It was the rest of what modern Halloween represented that was passionately resented by Alan. He had christened it "The Festival of Chav." He would speak to anyone who took the tima e to notice, whether an innocuous supermarket checkout assistant or passerby at the bus stop.

"Call me a snob and miserable fool, I just don't abide by the rule." Adding, "Why do people have to decorate houses, hedges and benches with cobwebs, ghosts and ghouls? It makes such a mess and eyesore. An utter blight to the landscape just to give some nincompoop a fright".

"Ridiculous and waste of money," and, "Have people more money than sense?" he discussed with Barny and Sid during lunchtime at the Centre.

Now he was in his element seething with annoyance about "The Festival of Chav". Imploring and cursing about trick or treat. How it was an opportunity for those pesky kids across the road a chance to torment an old man.

"In my day, it was called begging and you'd have been hit with a dustbin lid or clip around the earhole," he moaned to Debbie his lovely next-door neighbour.

One year, they had posted a fake dog turd and they had splattered his door with slime. He hadn't heard them knock or ring the bell.

"Where are their parents, or a policeman?" he implored, shaking with rage and fear, to Debbie.

He did try to get into the spirit, giving Debbie a bag of sweets and chocolates to share with her children. His bone of contention and nemesis were the adolescents who made his life a misery. He decided it was time to pay back.

"Greedy kids. I'll show them trick or treat," he told William, his son, on their weekly phone calls.

"I've bought some joke laxative chocolate."

He complained to Christine at the bank whilst drawing out his pension.

"Witches, ghouls, fancy dress. Mr Kipling fondant fancies in fluorescent green. Starbucks Spiced Pumpkin latte, expensive sugar rush. Plastic spiders, squidgy jelly eyes, what a surprise! It's insane"

Christine smiled and listened to his gripes, that continued:

"Fancy dress with hair and face in purple, orange, black and red. I'd like to stay in bed. It's a load of cheap Chinese manufactured tat to go to landfill and hyped. Is what I think of that. Utterly ludicrous tripe."

There was something magical about pumpkins, the sight of an organic set of fairy lights brightening dark autumn nights. From earth to plate, soup, seeds, and sustenance; recycled and renewed. Alan reneged on eating pumpkin soup and pie.

"You can't beat corned beef hash and Manchester tart. Proper grub, none of this American muck," he complained and looked at his warm bowl of pumpkin soup with disdain, deciding to eat just the complementary bread roll aside on a small plate.

"We'd heard about the Pendel witches, Lancaster Assizes and took William and his friends to Alderley Edge one October half term." He remembered fondly of memories from a long time ago, as his fellow diners concurred how different life had been.

"Folklore tales, Stig of the Dump and watching Scooby Doo, when William was a mere boy."

"Ghosts, ghouls, and apple bobbing."

"None of this mass consumption, a cultural reduction."

"Decorating your home for Halloween and celebrating, fair enough and nice to do."

Alan was in his soap box arguing the pros and cons of Halloween. No one was out of the firing line, including Wendy, Tracey and Miriam, the lunch assistants. They were dressed in Halloween costumes and had decorated the tables with bright lanterns, pumpkins, and vases of orange flowers. After lunch there was to be a screening of a black and white Peter Cushing film, with a slice of carrot cake and brew to end the day. They were determined to make the day entertaining for the residents.

"I accept," holding up his hands, "that it breaks up the drawing autumn nights and half term school holiday gloom. I am cynical and mean about Halloween. Apologies to those who are keen."

In his and fellow diners' day, their celebration had been Guy Fawkes night. Halloween was very much an afterthought. Penny for the guy. Spending the money on cheap beer and sneaky woodbines. Asking for old wood. Someone clearing out a house, "Would you mind taking that?" Bedsteads, tables, chairs, rabbit hutches. Doors, floorboards, a bit of dust and rust. Never daring to knock on doors. Autum half term and then Christmas countdown. Standing in front of a blazing bonfire on a wet miserable November night enveloped by an insidious cloud of mist, whilst adults perspired and prayed the rain held off. Burnt ashen raw baked potatoes, treacle toffee and sparklers, Catherine wheels. Rockets and bangers. Roman Candles. Burnt pan handles and grubby hands. Cascading purple, green, gold, technicolour showers.

Now Alan was currently waiting in Accident and Emergency, after slipping on pumpkin remnants strewn on a damp slippery pavement. Debbie had kindly dropped him off and only had to wait a mere ten hours for an x-ray.

"There is company, warmth, and more drama than on any soap or play. Best entertainment I've had for ages and saved on my fuel bills," he said to himself.

The sound of autumn showers on Hallowe'en echoed on the glass ceilings. Autumn was bedding in for winter and dark long hours. The curtain of summer was coming down after its final encore.

"It's been a nice night," he thought to himself and no pesky kids in sight.

"They have done me a favour leaving a trail of tat and pumpkin debris."

"How much compensation can I claim?".contemplating his options.

"No trip or fall" reciting the accident claims compensation firms.

Those adverts he watched on daytime television whilst watching Countdown, The Chase, and programmes of that ilk. He'd always fancied having a Stanna Stair lift installed, freedom of a mobility scooter and luxuriating in a whirlpool jacuzzi bath. Most of all he had the desire to travel far.

"This will come in nicely for my trip to visit William in Australia next spring."

"So much for trick or treat!"

Ba Humbug Halloween ...

STORIES
COUCH TO ROMANCE
Catherine Grant-Salmon

Casey had recently been for an over forties' health check at her local Medical Centre and needed to rectify the negative outcomes. She had attributed her increased weight and clothes getting tighter as due to the perimenopause and shrinking in the wash. Not Chardonnay and crisps, chocolate and cake. Wine o'clock and chocolate were essential commodities to add to her shopping list.

The practice nurse had spelt it out in no uncertain terms. Her blood pressure was high, cholesterol increased and borderline diabetes. Casey was shocked. It would be hard giving up her favourite tipples of a few glasses of Chardonnay or Rose and tucking into Cadbury's Dairy Milk. She loved dunking Hob Nobs and Chocolate digestives in a mug of frothy chocolate sprinkled Cappuccino whilst sitting in her Winnie the Pooh pyjamas. The intoxicating pleasure of removing her bra and make up free watching rubbish on television after a hard day at work. Weekends, any night, comfortable and chilling out. The gym filled her with dread, all those buffed skinny and toned bodies in Lycra and muscular monotone six-pack blokes pumping iron, the same with step aerobics and yoga.

She was exercise averse, always the last one to be chosen for a team sport at school and ridiculed for lack of athleticism. Memories of gnarled, rutted, muddy hockey pitches underneath windswept graphite-grey skylines and the stench of boiled cabbage and onions permeating the air. Set behind a distopian concrete school block. Cold, chapped, purplish-blue legs, wearing a short shirt, aertex polo shirt and matching navy-blue knickers. Shivering, gibbering nervous wreck. She yearned to stay safely indoors, absorbed in a book or concentrating on her artwork of watercolours and a few sketches. Not enforced solitude and no gratitude for her endeavours; fed in sodden clothes to the leeches, whose undercurrents of threatening taunts to haunt into their lair. Compulsory Physical Education – the words stood out on each timetable. How many fake notes she had written to be excused from games due to periods every week or so?

Then one night, while aimlessly scrolling on Facebook, was an advert from the local Health Improvement team. Saturday morning running group for beginners at Warburton Park. 'Reach your goal of couch to five kilometres in ten weeks. Free to join.'v Casey tried to ignore the advertisement that kept appearing on her feed, poking a reminder and nudging until she budged off her sofa.

"Well, I suppose it might be worth going along" she nervously told her work colleague, Edwin.

"I'll sponsor you a tenner a mile," he replied.

"No pressure then, make it ten minutes for a tenner," she joked "and please keep it quiet from the rest of the office," convinced that she'd fail and didn't want to look stupid.

The only exercise she had done in recent years was running for a bus to work and too tired to do anything on her return.

Warburton Park was on the quiet side of town with a graffiti-strewn Victorian bandstand, tennis courts and café. Flower beds, clusters of Rhododendrons and pine trees. Dog walkers, litter pickers, skateboarding youths. Football games, toddlers throw and catch with a bright coloured ball. Casey would have loved to have played on the swings, slide and climbing frame. Instead of learning how to run in the cold damp grey skies. She longed to hide under the duvet, snuggly and warm.

"I really must be as mad as a hatter and have nothing to lose. Just give it a try to say that I've been and it's not for me. Skipping the odd glass of wine and chocolate would suffice" she told herself with trepidation on the way to the park, having rummaged in the back of her wardrobe for a pair of unused trainers and scruffy joggers. "I'm not wasting money on buying any kit. This will do," she decided for the training session. "I'll probably be hopeless as ever at sport."

At the beginning running was arduous, five or ten minutes at a time. Gary, the enthusiastic trainer encouraged the group to do better as the days grew wetter, and the curtain of summer dropped down into autumn. Dark clouds, rain, sleet and wind.

"I really must be bonkers," she thought, tripping over wet conkers in mulch-soaked trainers with joggers sticking to her legs. Exhausted, bedraggled tired and sore.

STORIES

"Casey, well done, you've just run a mile," Gary encouragingly said.

Jubilant and euphoric with legs like lead, she'd reached a target beyond her dreams. Edwin reached for his wallet to give her the promised ten pounds.

"Well done, I will double it, twenty pounds for two miles, and thirty for three etcetera," he said.

Casey decided to donate the money to charity. The payoff she was getting was in feeling fit and satisfied with her achievements.

"There is a Parkrun, as a finale to the course."

Gary encouraged the group to sign up and "everyone welcome on Saturday mornings" he announced at their final session. "See you all next week."

The running sessions were now part of Casey's routine and she didn't hesitate to sign up for the park run. It was no longer a chore to get out of bed without a hangover and discarded takeaway.

"Oi, watch where you are going" she overheard someone shout.

Nonchalantly looking around and skipping through puddles. Mud splattered and exhilarated.

"I said watch out for my dog," the person groaned.

Casey was in a world of her own; bird sounds and wind in her hair, running through crunchy, crinkly leaves.

"Selfish runners, inconsiderate fools," they blasphemed in exasperation, as she kicked a yelping bundle of tan fluff.

"What do you think you are doing? You've hurt my Pixie," he continued in a raised angry voice "this park is for everyone to enjoy, not just you and your pals," he nastily insinuated and pointed at her, "it's bad enough with all the cyclists, not ringing their bells, getting in the way and making a nuisance."

Casey's hand covered her mouth.

"I've been trying to get your attention to watch out for my dog for the past few minutes and you didn't take any notice," the stranger implored as Casey stood frozen, heart beating, on the spot with tears welling in her eyes.

"I... I really I am so, so sorry," she stuttered an apology.

Shortly hearing a yapping bark from the tan fluff near her feet, as it was scooped up into the arms of the concerned giant of a man who smiled at this beloved pooch.

"There, there my baby. Daddy loves you. " It licked his face.

"Is your dog, ok?" Casey enquired, "I'll pay for any vet's fees if it's hurt. Promise. Honestly, my fault. Should look where I was going."

She felt humiliated by his passive aggressive demeanour. Boomeranged back to painful memories of school bullies associated with its connotations of flailing limbs, hockey sticks, breaking bones and deliberate obstruction. Last one to finish in the Cross Country, embarrassed and red in the face. Not the confident runner she had become in ten weeks.

"Come on Casey, are you carrying on?" shouted the others.

"Yes, in a moment." She needed to talk to the stranger with his tiny dog, resplendent in a cerise and diamante collar and matching bow.

"This is Pixie, my Pomeranian, goes with me everywhere" as he introduced himself, "My name is Jake."

"Err, nice to meet you, sorry about tripping over Pixie" said Casey, "She's cute."

Jake stroked Pixie as he continued "Me favourite girl" who looked adoringly at her owner with angelic warm eyes. "Gives me unconditional love and affection. Sleeps curled up on the pillow beside me in bed and gives me a prod when I snore," adding, " Only the best will do for Pixie Dixie" Mellowing as he eulogised, Pixie was a tiny twinkling star gently plucked from a frosty moonlit sky.

"I really must be going and want to finish my run," Casey said as time was pressing and her limbs were getting stiff "There's a café near the bandstand, are you okay to wait?" adding, "I want to make sure you and Pixie are fine."

Jake responded, "Yes of course, enjoy the rest of your run." She played along with his changing mood and pleasantness, catching up

STORIES

soon with the others, mud-splattered, sweating and out of breath floating the rest of the course.

"Congratulations, your best time so far," Gary cheered. "No one will ever dare take me back to that awful time again," she said to herself, empowered with anger running through her veins.

"See you later, unless you have other plans?" Gary had noticed the earlier altercation and amicable parting. Jake won't woo me that easily she thought as she met him in the café for a fresh orange juice, giving Pixie a warm cuddle. They swapped numbers. Was romance in the air? She mumbled sweet nothings in Jake's ear as they left side by side with Pixie as happy as can be.

"Nice to meet you Pixie" as she stroked the dog and bid farewell. "Jake quick word... don't try and hoodwink me, why wasn't Pixie on a lead? You had seen all the runners and were too busy looking on your phone." She questioned, "Thanks for your number. It'll come in handy if I've hurt myself later," concluding on her way to meet up with Jenny and Evan who were giving her a lift to an art exhibition.

"It's taken me years to feel this good about myself," she told Gary and Edwin later in the gym about Jake "You must be kidding. Would I really want to share my bed with man who sleeps with his dog and she's his favourite girl? I'd rather have a Cadbury's Twirl as a special treat after my run. This is so much fun and I just decided to sign up for Boxercise class."

The encounter with Jake in the park had been an alarm call. It was now time to channel her anger and rage for all those nightmarish times at school. Exorcise the demons and ghosts once and for all.

AN INTERESTING EXPERIENCE

CATHERINE GRANT-SALMON

Writing Challenge:
Tell of an interesting experience

One night, at the beginning of the September term. Gavin had accidentally walked into the wrong class at his local college and found himself enrolled on a life coaching course. Much to his consternation! Having planned to attempt learning holiday French, not that he had any intention of visiting France, he needed the challenge of mastering a new subject and people, striking up conversations with fellow students, as they mastered the machinations of linguistic extrapolation. An eclectic mix of characters from all walks of life and a great way to socialise. There was the usual demographic, from those with an A4 folder to a single piece of torn note pad. Pencil cases, highlighter pens in fluorescent yellow, magenta, acidic green and orange. Post-it notes, pencils and rubbers. They were intent to learn and absorb knowledge. Inquisitive, lonely, bored. They were a collective mish mash.

Gavin had mastered calligraphy, basket weaving, reiki, tai chi, and computer programming. There was so much to choose from the lengthy list of interesting subjects on offer to adult learners. His job in a call centre was mundane and interaction with the outside world was limited to a quick walk to the café at lunch time. In the winter months, he felt like a battery hen cooped up in a claustrophobic office. Depressing and summer daylight, an evening walk uplifting.

Patricia, the tutor was an eccentric lady with a pierced nose, ginger afro, who wore kaftans and silver bovver boots. She had previously self-identified as a tea pot and, currently, an Aspidistra.

Nobody in the group managed, in the entire ten weeks, to grasp exactly what life coaching was all about. Other than segmenting and colouring in a drawn circle into eight, labelling each one with a part of your life needing improvement on a scale of one to ten, it was like a game of Trivial Pursuit! How many pieces of coloured pie in a drunken haze? Patricia's teaching was ad hoc, saying she was guided by the spirits. Gin, Vodka, Bacardi came to mind.

STORIES

Anyway, it was an evening out for Gavin, and having hated school, informal relaxed learning was a pleasure without pressure.

The group was soon reduced from the enthusiastic newbies, heading for the gym in January. The predictability of a rhetorical new start, and life plans. Fitness regimes, diets, and beginners' origami. Evening classes sorted out the learners from the shirkers, or with nothing better to do. One week, they'd been asked to make a collage of their life! A few sticks, toffee wrappers and bottle tops were supposed to be interpreted into a meaningful masterpiece.

In the sopheric incense-smoked tumbleweed of week six or seven, Patricia threw a curve ball by announcing to the class she would like them to share an interesting experience. Everyone sat silent, looking ominously at one another and waited with bated breath to see who would dare go first. They would be setting the standard. Hazel the traffic warden jumped in and eulogised about putting a ticket on David Beckham's Bentley. Mike said that he had swum with dolphins in Madagascar. Jude played the flute bare foot at Glastonbury. Barry planted radishes on Lindisfarne. Patricia nodded and smiled, talking about roads and journeys.

"Gavin, what you like to share?" she enquired.

Put on the spot, all that was missing was a bright light shining into his face being interrogated. "Pass!" would have been a great answer. Perspiring, panic-stricken and mouth dry, he had not done anything so interesting in his life, so tried to avoid the question.

Mike gave him a gentle nudge. "It's okay mate," he whispered, "I've never been to Madagascar or swum with dolphins. I made it all up. Read about it whilst waiting for a dental appointment."

Patricia, who was getting impatient with Gavin, asked again, "What is your interesting life experience?"

Gavin paused and started talking to the group.

"There are none. I've never swam with dolphins, trekked the Andes, visited the Taj Mahal; foreign travel, wrestling in gravel and painting parrots. Interesting experiences to me, are not highlights or written words. I've not played trombone in a brass band, managed a dogs' home or had a hydrangea named after me. I don't have a passport and visited only one capital city where they speak a foreign language - Holyhead. It's the mundanities and vagaries of human nature that are interesting experiences, no two days are the same commuting or walking round my local park. Seasons and people change. It's the small things that matter. Choosing books at the library; talking to the bank cashiers and listening to the radio. Interesting experiences are subjective and like to hear how much joy these bring to another. I like observing and interacting with people on buses, trains, pubs. Rugby League and Salford City F.C. This is the fabric of life; interesting experiences are second to none. You can find out so much from talking to a stranger in a pub, library, or chiropodist. Supermarket checkouts and banks. Use your imagination and absorb in a book. People are important and valued, experiences and treasures rolled into one."

Patricia hesitated and looked at her watch, "My solar plexus is vibrating and I experience a lovely orange aura, Gavin. Cheerio. Must dash. I have a date with a stick of celery aka wife Claudia. Bring a horse chestnut or a rainbow for homework next week. Or poetry."

Deadly silence and forced contained sniggers followed.

"Anyone fancy going to the pub?" Barry enquired to the group.

"Yes defo," they all replied.

"Quiz and Karaoke on tonight, treat you all to a bag of pork scratchings at the Pig and Trumpet."

Now that is an interesting experience.

STORIES

THE JEWELLERY BOX

CATHERINE GRANT-SALMON

It was a cold dark winter morning as Mary began to wake up from yet another disturbed night's sleep, the joys of the menopause or the change as her mother would have described it as a woman's problem. She looked at her alarm clock and realised that it was still quite early, although daylight seemed a long time off. She snuggled into the warmth of her duvet for a few moments more.

She hated the long days and nights, as the clocks went back. Trick or Treat and Halloween in late October. There was no 'trick or treat' just the end of summertime. As it seemed that everywhere became dark and grey: not even the twinkling bright lights at Christmastime improved her mood. She felt weighted down thanks to the dark enveloping days that permeated every pore of her soul. She could not see the beauty in the hedgerows of birds gathering grubs, bright red berries, and crisp icy haw frost or feel the scrunch and joy of walking through autumn leaves as nature shed its skin. Mary yearned to escape from this cocoon of glum, as her tired body ached for warmth and sunshine, she longed for brighter days ahead. Winter seemed endless, unlike her alarm clock that was jolting her out of her slumbers and another day.

As Mary opened her bedroom curtains, wrapping herself in her crimson red dressing gown to keep warm, she was transfixed by a silvery, shining crescent moon tinged with frost, seemingly looking directly at her, as if saying "mother nature isn't so bad after all."

She paused for a moment at its simplistic awe-inspiring beauty. To think a man has walked on the moon. What a remarkable achievement; who could have imagined it? She remembered watching the landing on Mum and Dad's old black and white three channels television in their council flat. Apollo, Astronauts Neil Armstrong, and Buzz Aldrin; the Space age seemed so futuristic then. Ziggy Stardust: Life on Mars and the Clangers from a distant magical planet.

Mary had cared for her mum Val after her dad had passed away in the nineteen eighties. Now with some reluctance Val had moved into a retirement care home called "Sycamore Place" in a scenic part of town with all mod cons. This was being paid for by Mary's brother David. Val was so proud of her son's achievements and dismissed Mary as the dutiful daughter. All the arrows of good fortune had pointed to David or so it seemed to Mary. In Val's eyes he could do no wrong. Mary wasn't envious of her brother. He had worked hard and she was grateful for him paying for Val's care, as her health had deteriorated and she needed a walking cane.

Since moving into *Sycamore Place,* Val had become fastidious about her appearance and the cane was no exception. She had chosen a florescent pink and silver glitter cane, bringing out her inner *Strictly* with bling and glamour. The singer Frankie Vaughan with his cane and top hat wouldn't have been out of place.

"I don't want any old cane, which is beige or drab, it's a fashion accessory," implied Val indignantly to Mary and the occupational health therapist.

Instead of a walking stick, to her disdain, which she badly needed, the cane's brightness would make sure she would be noticed by everyone at Sycamore Place.

Later in the morning, Mary went to visit her mum and always made sure to be there while it was still daylight. They were able to sit in the conservatory with a brew and chat, overlooking the manicured gardens. She observed a squirrel foraging for leftovers under a bird table and blackbirds flitting from tree to tree. How the wildlife kept the residents amused and a nice distraction for the visitors who came to the home. There was the chance of something outside to awaken a memory if only for a minute or so. The key to consciousness mattered so much to them. Sycamore Place was lovely and welcoming, Val had done well to get a place there so soon.

Mary was quietly contemplating Mum's new surroundings. How different they were from their sparce and homely council flat. Val returned from her room carrying a jewellery box which Mary had never seen. It was battered with faded harlequin patterns and, as Val gently opened its lid, a delicate ballerina with alabaster skin and tattered, pale pink tutu began to dance to the tune of Tchaikovsky's Nutcracker ballet. Val's eyes welled with tears and then turned to

STORIES

the back of the box and opened a hidden drawer. Mary was transfixed as Val brought out a photograph of a young couple in masks and needed to hold her shaking hand. On the back was written, *Darling Val, your devoted pen friend Jan, Antwerp 1956.*

For those few moments, Val was not in an expensive care home with all mod cons. She was a fun-loving teenager on an exchange visit to post war-torn Europe. Her first trip to the continent eating *escargot* and *pommes frites* instead of bread and jam and Spam. There had been a magnetic attraction with her Belgian beau, away from the bleakness of home. *Rock Around The Clock* blasted out of the Juke Box - and Elvis too. Not medication time.

Mary was perplexed and wondered what had brought those memories coming back. Where had the jewellery box suddenly appeared from? What other secrets had Val been hiding from her?

They gently walked back to Val's downstairs cheerful bedroom looking out at the grounds: with her favourite photos, cushions, duvet cover and blanket, radio, and table lamp. These were reminders of sharing her council flat with Mary and their dog Bert, a Doberman crossed by Whippet. What a handful Bert had been or was that her husband? and the dog was called Eric? One way or another they were from the same time of her life and neither was house trained. Mary noticed on her mum's bookshelf amongst the *Catherine Cooksons* and *Mills and Boons,* was a globe. Val walked gingerly over and pointed out to a place on the globe, hesitating then opened her mouth to speak. These words Mary could not comprehend as Val said, "That's where David works".

It was South America not Dubai or Abu Dhabi as Mary had been led to believe by both. David's work was very different to what Mary had understood it to be. She realised something sinister was a foot and that is how he had paid for Val's expensive care costs with all mod cons in luxurious accommodation in a scenic part of town. Did her mother know this too and was she complicit in his actions? Were there other secrets or seeds of doubt for Mary to find out about as the keys of consciousness unlocked memories in the ether of her mother's mind.

TEACUP

Catherine Grant-Salmon

I have been donated by Suzy and now reside at Millie's Tea Shop on the quiet side of town, beside the ladies' boutiques, hairdressers, and parish church.

Suzy's gran was my first owner, a pearl wedding present in nineteen sixty-four. She treasured me with pride and joy in her mahogany display cabinet, alongside sherry glasses, decanter, and heirlooms. We proudly took our place, a china tea service, white with silver rim and decorated with a pattern of swirling feathers and Fleur D Lys design in the centre. There are six each of us medium size cups and saucers with matching side plates. I have come with good repute, fine bone china made in Worcestershire with a crest to boot. My official title is *Royal Worcestershire Silver Chantily 1963*. I am delicate to touch and make a gentle tinkling sound when poured with tea and returned to saucer. My handle is fine and sturdy with a simple line of silver along my spine and scalloped edges. We also have an accompanying tea pot and milk jug with sugar bowl to complete the set. Gran saved up to buy a matching cake stand and silver server with Green Shield Stamps, later clawed tongs for sugar lumps. Grandad treated her to silver teaspoons and imitation pearl necklace on their anniversary.

She loved how we all shone on display in the cabinet aside the family photos like the ornaments on the mantlepiece and sideboard. In her sitting room, or 'parlour' as she liked to say. Brought out for special occasions from christenings to engagements and wakes. The circle of life, encapsulated in bone china, from cradle to the grave. We were a sense of class and respect, standards to behold. "More tea, Vicar?" and polite conversation, introductions, awkwardness, and rituals. Best suits and dresses composed and amused. Gentle sips to imbue, of Ceylon tea and wanting a *proper brew* of strong builders' tea in a mug. Grandad kept a tot of whisky in his silver hip-flask to surreptitiously pass around.

Now I am here in Millie's on a nice replica Welsh dresser with polished wood and gentle curves. Suzy wanted to keep us but her

STORIES

flat is far too small and modern. There is a fake *Clarisse Cliffe* design tea set beside us in garish *Art Deco* colours. An *Eternal Beau* eighties post-menopausal divorce completes the tea sets. We are accompanied by an esoteric brown and ochre patterned Hornsea coffee pot and cups from vintage nineteen seventies style. Our sets are quite eclectic from different decades and lovingly tendered hand-me-downs from a forgotten distant past. Millie likes to do her best, the tearoom is cosy and warm with pictures of sunflowers and cats. Vases of flowers and bee cushions. Classical music and jazz. The sound of a pendulum clock and a pot dray horse and carriage.

Welcoming comfort from a hubbub of chaos and noise with touches of quirkiness.

I love to hear the customers say, "Shall I be mother?" as they pour a brew. Assam, Darjeeling, Earl Grey is filled in me. Camomile and good old Yorkshire tea with just a splash of milk. No sugar lumps, sweeteners of course and watching calories. I am daintily held and drank from with pursed lips of coral, rose or crimson red. Millie likes to decorate her side plates with delicate ornate doilies in pink and white. There is gold for Christmas with a mince pie and cracker. Her cakes are quite simple fare, always a Victoria Sponge, Eccles Cakes and scones with jam and cream. She will dress up tables with balloons and flowers and ask her friend, who is good with modelling fondant, to ice one of her Victoria sponges. Glasses of Prosecco to toast good news and celebrations whilst conjuring an evocation of nostalgia.

We are privy to pleasant conversations, joy, laughter and gossip as brief interludes to the mundanities of daily life. Hopes and fears, support and tears as comforting hands are held and tissue given. If only cups could tell and impart, their wisdom is second to none. I am a connection and social interaction, warming and consoling wrapped into one.

DAVID'S SYSTEM

Catherine Grant-Salmon

I had this system for getting exactly what I wanted from people, beginning at primary school. By exploiting the most vulnerable in our class, for a few pennies, a thruppenny bit, silver tanner or mega bucks shilling tuck shop money. I didn't care how much that had cost their parents' weekly family household budget. They could miss out on a Wagonwheel, Jammy Dodger, piece of toast or Milky Way. I made quite a killing for writing a few wrong answers in their exercise books. They thought I was bright and clever. Fools they didn't know.

I was nine and a half to be precise; they still believed in Father Christmas. I had found out by listening to Mum and Dad talking late at night on my way to the outside privy. There was no such person. How much can I get from them to keep quiet and not tell my younger sister Mary? Maybe two or three years. She's not that bright and, I also promised to stop wetting the bed at night.

They were all the same, I decided, the stupid ones at school. A bribe of what I wanted in exchange for not making them look like fools. How many wrong sums and adverbs I pretended to know, and they thought I was great, smart, and popular. "David Robert's you'll go far," Miss Johnson our teacher used to say. Others looked in awe; the ones with scabby knees, scuffed shoes, hand-me-downs and picked their noses. Jam-caked around their half-asleep faces from a snatched grab of toast while mums rushed them to school and then off to the factory to work an hour or so. I'll make a killing out of them, fool's gold, and that's how it all began for me.

"Stop looking at me in the playground, you creep, leech., was the time Lesley called me a leech for the first of many times. I had met my match and liked her. She was in the class above and had a long blonde ponytail; smart uniform and wore pillar box red shiny Mary Jane shoes. She played rounders on the school field, knew how to catch a ball, and ran fast. She played the recorder and guitar - unheard of by us mere mortals with the triangles at back. I was in awe; she was a star in my eyes.

STORIES

"How much have you got this week?" When taken to one side hidden behind the caretakers prefab cabin, "That'll do nicely – half your takings from the fool's gold," thanks Lesley.

Behind me, in the corner of my eye was someone else, a boy I'd seen from sir's class, waiting his turn with the lovely Lesley, stirrings of pre-pubescent lust.

I realised then that this was a primary example of how exploitation works and was answerable to its machinations all along at school where it all began. There is always someone mightier in the system who would prove to be my cost in life.

THE MEETING

LORRAINE TATTERSALL

Billy was 50 and single, and as yet had not met anyone he could settle down with. He wasn't perfect by any means and chose to wear a riser in a shoe to hide a limp. His eyesight wasn't too clever either so he wore contact lenses if he went out on a date instead of his glasses, even though they made his eyes sore after use. All in the name of vanity his sister would say, why can't you just be yourself, there isn't anyone out there as kind, thoughtful and respectful as you and one day you will meet someone who will see those qualities and not your limp or bad eyes. But Billy was not too sure of that.

Then one night he sat at his computer on a dating site recommended to him. After looking through the first few pages, he came across a lady that ticked all his boxes: 45, single, outgoing, friendly, reliable and with a good sense of humour – just what he was looking for. After some thought , he clicked on the 'Interested' button and after a few weeks of messaging the pair decided to meet in the restaurant of a nearby trendy Boutique Hotel.

Billy had his best suit cleaned; then starched and ironed his white shirt, polished his shoes, and took his time shaving and grooming for this special meeting, whilst at the same time across town, the lady was taking her time to look her best too.

On arrival, he was shown to his table and promptly, with his mouth so dry, ordered a drink and sat nervously sipping the glass of overpriced bottled water, anxiously waiting for 7.30 pm, their agreed meeting time. Bang on the dot, the double doors of the dining room opened and in walked – or should one say, sashayed across the floor – a vision. How to describe this lady walking towards him? She was at least 5 foot 10 or 11 inches tall. "It's a good job, I'm over 6 foot tall," Billy thought, as she seated herself before him. She had long, blonde hair, azure blue eyes enhanced by thick black lashes. Her teeth were pearly white; not those that were too white for your mouth and could almost dazzle you in the dark, but just perfect when she smiled. She wore ruby red lipstick that he noticed matched her

STORIES

long talon-like fingernails as they shook hands. She looked very elegant in her long grey silk dress. Very tasteful jewellery, finished off with a silver bag and matching six inch-heeled strappy shoes.

Billy swallowed, thinking it was a good job he had brought his credit card; having a feeling this lady could be high maintenance. Once they were both settled, he indicated to the waiter to bring over the menu and wine list. They had a brilliant night, talking and laughing, and it felt as though they were old friends – so comfortable in one another's company. Billy was pleasantly surprised when he asked for the bill and found that the choice of food the lady had chosen was one of the cheapest and she hadn't gone for one of the more expensive dishes. The same with her drink, preferring a glass of lime and soda rather than the designer wines that were so popular with the ladies of the day.

They were the last to leave the restaurant but managed to order a brandy and coffee to take into the lounge for a nightcap. Both were sorry when the evening came to an end, but end it must. Billy offered to pay for a taxi to take the lady home and was surprised when she said it wasn't necessary as she had booked a room in the hotel for the night. Something she thought best to do just in case her date did not match up to her expectations and she had to make a quick exit. But Billy had turned out to be everything she could ask for in a man.

He escorted her to the lift, promising to keep in touch and that their next meet – or date, he corrected – would be sooner rather than later. As she entered the lift, she flashed him one of her beaming smiles – one he would not forget – and replied, "Maybe!"

Billy walked home on cloud nine, thinking how lucky he was that this living doll had come into his life. He found it hard to sleep, but when eventually did it wasn't for long. After tossing and turning, he got up, and over a cup of coffee decided he would go back to the hotel and present the lady with a bunch of flowers to thank her for a lovely evening. Upon arrival, the receptionist said that it must be one special lady to be receiving such beautiful blooms. His "blooms," he replied she was and went on to describe her.

After ringing the breakfast area to enquire if such a lady was there and being told, "No," she rang housekeeping to ask if they could check vacated bedrooms even though nobody fitting the lady's description had checked out of the hotel earlier.

Shortly afterwards, housekeeping rang back to say there was something rather odd and could somebody come up to take a look. The receptionist asked Billy to accompany her, seeing he was connected to the person who had occupied it. Upon entering, the said bedroom the receptionist looked startled but not as much as Billy and patted him on the shoulder before leaving. Billy made his way to the bed looking down on neatly arranged items: a long blonde wig; false black eyelashes; and a box containing contact lenses of the same azure blue as his lady friend's eyes. A ruby red lipstick and matching jar of nail polish stood on the bedside cabinet with long red fingernails scattered about with jewellery that was not as expensive as he thought, realising they were made of paste. A padded bra and briefs were draped over a chair with silver shoes and silver bag on it and a grey silk dress hung on a wardrobe door.

Surely any minute now he would wake up and find himself snuggled up in his own bed but it wasn't a dream, it was all too real. By now, he should be handing over flowers instead of being surrounded by a lady's cast-offs. So trying to understand why she had done what she had, he made his way to the lift.

At that moment, a neat, trim, mousy-haired lady, wearing old fashioned attire, was finishing her coffee in the dining room. After putting on her glasses to find the right coinage, she tipped the waiter then left without anyone giving her a second glance. Crossing the foyer she dropped her keys into the box at the reception desk just as the lift doors opened and out walked Billy. He almost collided with this lady as he walked towards the reception desk intending to gift the flowers to the receptionist. Taking a long, hard look before apologising he heard the receptionist ask if the lady had had a comfortable stay and hoped she would come back again soon. He was startled when the lady replied, in a familiar voice, saying "Maybe!" and could she pick up the items left in the room at a later time. She flashed them both a beaming smile as she headed for the revolving door and before he could react, she had jumped into a waiting taxi.

STORIES

The moral of this tale is: remember all of you like Billy out there, beauty and glamour are not everything. It's what comes from within that count just like the lady's smile, warmth and sense of humour. Her name was Sam by the way and, as for you Billy, Sam saw you for all your finer points so forget the shoe riser and contact lenses and just be you. I hope Billy makes contact again, don't you?

POPPY'S TONGUE

Lorraine Tattersall

"Hello, Poppy," no reply, "Oh, dear, have you lost your tongue?" still no response. "Well I'd best go and see where you've lost it, shall I?" said Grandma, setting off to find it.

First place she went to was school. "Hello, Grandma," said the teacher looking up from marking her pupils' work "What can I do for you?"

"Well, I was wondering if Poppy had left her tongue here today as she seems to have lost it."

"Oh, that's sad, it's not here - it was very much in action as she left school with her friends; you could try the shop as sometimes they stop there for a treat on the way home."

"Thank you, Mrs Jones, I will do that."

The doorbell rang as Grandma entered the shop; the owner was engaged in putting newspapers into bags for his paper boys to collect and deliver.

"Hello, Grandma, come for a paper?"

"No, but will take one whilst I'm here; I've come to see if Poppy came in today after school as she has lost her tongue and I'm trying to trace it."

The shopkeeper thought hard and then shook his head, "No, sorry, I've not seen her today but you could try the park; I did see some little ones going in there earlier."

"Oh, dear, thank you anyway, I will head there now."

"Hello, Grandma" said the Park Keeper, "come for a go on the swings?" he laughingly asked.

"I wish but no, I've come to see if Poppy was here earlier only she's lost her tongue and I was wondering if it was here."

Scratching his head, he replied "Sorry, no – I've picked up lots of litter but unfortunately no tongues. You could try MacDonald's, that's very popular with the kiddies"

STORIES

"Thank you, I'll call there next."

Pushing open the door of MacDonald's the smell made Grandma's tummy rumble as it was well past her teatime.

"Hello, would you like to order?" asked the waitress.

"No, tempting as it is, I've come to see if a tongue has been handed in as my granddaughter seems to have lost hers."

"Oh, what a shame, I will go and look in the Lost Property, you would be surprised at what people leave."

A few minutes later the waitress was back. "Sorry, lots of umbrellas, hats and gloves but no tongues."

"Oh, well, thanks for your help anyway."

Wearingly, walking back up her avenue a thought came to Grandma. The car, I bet it's there! So, opening the car door, she started looking under seats, in the glove box and even checked the boot just in case but nothing. Only a few sweet wrappers, crisp packets, empty and half-empty drink cartons but no tongues.

"Any luck?" asked Poppy's dad, when Grandma entered the house.

"No, I've been everywhere. I will just see how she is and if she's got it back"

"Well, I've not heard a peep out of her whilst you've been gone."

As Grandma entered the lounge, Poppy was still sat comfortably on the sofa playing on her i-Pad just as she was when Grandma left.

"Well, have you found that tongue of yours, yet?" Grandma asked. Poppy looked up and shook her head.

"Oh, well, I'll just have a cuppa and then we'll have to inform the police and they can put out an appeal. I bet it will be on the front page of the newspapers tomorrow and we need to tell school too as you will not be able to sing in the show without a tongue. Such a pity, after all that hard work you've put in it looks like your best friend Crystal will have to take your place."

With that news, Poppy looked up startled and as Grandma went to go through the door she heard a sound.

"Was that you, Poppy?" she asked laughingly "you little minx, was it in your mouth all the time?"

Poppy nodded then started talking ten to the dozen like she normally did. Grandma sat down pulling Poppy into her arms and thought, "Perfect – I would not want you any other way."

STORIES

GHOST'S STORY.

PAULINE MITCHELL

I'm a ghost. I used to be a person but then I died.

I did not want to die, in fact my previously unhappy life was beginning to look up when I suddenly died, crossing a road. I don't know what happened, but all of a sudden, my body kind of collapsed, all life came to an end. I have been trying to find out why.

And that's why I hang around. I'm not ready to be dead, even though I was wrapped up, stuck in a box and the lid nailed down, and my body disappeared. Now the me inside the box could somehow escape and return if I felt like it.

So I wander round the place where it happened. But the strange thing is people's reaction. They either don't believe I'm real, or they are frightened! What do they think I can do to them?

That day, the day that I died, started like any other. My older brother shouted at me, calling me a lazy eipehound– I hadn't cooked his breakfast so he tore up my homework books. I was late for school – again. And got into trouble – again. I was angry with him but couldn't think how to stop his bullying. I was quiet all day, but my mind kept returning to the injustice. He was bullying me and I was powerless. My mother was an invalid, staying in bed till the carer came.

Arthur was out at work. His work was poorly paid, so he had to work many long hours.

My unhappy day crept by. Lessons were difficult – I wasn't clever and struggled with maths and science, and the teachers couldn't make their lessons meaningful to me.

At last the bell rang for the end of the school day. I picked up my coat, checked my bag for all the homework, and walked with my friend out of the school. We chatted – she understood how things at home were for me and was always sympathetic.

Suddenly my brother joined us, bullying and saying hurtful things – I was ugly, stupid and a bad cook.

He said I only had one friend. And she was ugly, he said.

My friend became very angry with him and started to shout at him. He hit her, hard, across her face, and I lost my temper and punched him hard. He swung his schoolbag at my head and I fell into the road just as a bus was passing.

When I awoke my body was floating away from me, my friend was weeping hysterically, my brother was screaming at me and the street was filled with people, all looking horrified.

Then I fell asleep.

When I awoke my body was tightly confined in a box and being lowered into a hole. Nobody heard my calls for help.

But my spirit lives on, searching for the people I called family and friends, and the enemies who ended my life. I seek them still though many years have passed. When I show myself to living people they mostly scream or run away. They seem to fear me – but I can't hurt them. Not now. And they don't stay long enough to let me explain what happened. My body is not with me – this shadow is all there is of me. And it is deeply troubled.

STORIES

ABANDONED

Veronica Scotton

Nora was drinking black tea and watching Lorraine Kelly when a "Hello Nanna" rang in her ears. Her granddaughter "bless" she never missed a day calling on her way home from work. Sometimes the visits were short and sweet "just checking you're OK" and other times "I'll put the kettle on, I've got news for you" when she would sit for an hour or so gossiping and chatting, Nora lived for these times.

This time, as Rachael gave her a hug and kiss on the cheek, Nora noticed the glow on her granddaughter's cheeks, "Have you got something to tell me Rach'?"

"Nanna, you are a witch!"

"You're expecting, aren't you?"

"Yes, but don't tell Mum just yet, you know how she frets and worries, let it be our secret until after the 12-week scan."

Later when the carer came to help her into bed, she asked her to buy some wool. Her hands were arthritic and her eyes not so good, but she would knit a matinee jacket for her great-grandchild if it was the last thing she did.

A week later the back of the jacket was complete and she casted on the stitches for a sleeve as she watched The Chase. She was feeling a bit tired, which was quite common those days. She remembered a time when she had managed on less than four hours sleep a night when her children were babies, but that was 60 years ago she remembered, when a strong cup of coffee would be sufficient to make it through the day.

She felt like she could hear her heart beating slowly in her chest and rubbed her arms that were aching more than usual. Putting the needles tidily together and laying them on the coffee table, Nora closed her eyes and quickly fell asleep listening to Bradley Walsh commiserating with the latest victim of The Beast.

In the dream Nora felt alive and energetic but confused with the dream because she seemed to be floating in the air, she could see the top of a very old person's head. With a shock she realised that the person she could see was herself, "Was this what it was like to be dead?"

The next evening when she let herself in to see Nanna, Rachael suspected nothing, the TV was playing and she called out a breezy "Hi Nanna, I've brought some Eccles cakes, your favourites." The cakes were forgot as she saw the strange pallor of her beloved grandmother. Falling asleep with the gas fire blazing had already started the rigor mortis, she went to hug her nana and jumped back in shock at the cold hard cheeks. With shaking hands, she dialled 999, and then her mother. The child in her womb moved for the first time and she hardly noticed.

It took hours for the paramedics and police to complete their checks, then the family called to say goodbye to the lovely matriarch of the family. The knitting lay abandoned and unnoticed as tea was drunk and hearts broke.

Weeks later, following the burial, Helen put her mother's house up for sale and began the brutal task of emptying all the contents. After the family and friends had chosen items that they wanted, the remaining contents were put into piles for the tip, the charity shop or to be sold on Amazon (her brother's idea). She picked up the knitting and wondered what to do with it. No one in the family had ever shown any interest in learning the skill. She wondered who her mother had been knitting for, and rolled the wool and pattern together and put it to one side until she could find out. But it was in the back of a drawer in her bedroom and forgotten by the time Elenora (to be called Nel and not Nora) was born.

Twenty years later after Helen had died after a long illness, Rachael was emptying her mother's house and like her mother before came across the knitting. A thought crossed her mind that perhaps this must have been her grandmother's because her mum had never been inclined to knit (Why would she, when baby clothes were cheap and cheerful?). But for the same reason as her mum, she couldn't find a place to give it to, would the charity shop be interested in an unfinished matinee coat?

But when Nel saw the knitting, she picked it up and it felt comfortable in her hands. She found a YouTube site that showed how to knit. She hadn't told anyone about the foetus growing in her womb. This jacket would be something special and personal she would never know that she was the reincarnation of her namesake, and that the knitting was what had been abandoned in her past life.

FRANK THE PAINTER

VERONICA SCOTTON

Writing Challenge:	
Protagonist: Frank the Painter	His Aim: To be Wild and Free
Obstacle: The Inspector	Action: Buys a new wardrobe

Frank The Painter! – wherever had that nickname come from? He didn't even enjoy painting, but the care home had all these new-fangled ideas, giving the residents jobs to keep dementia at bay. He'd been given the task of assisting the caretaker once and because he had made a reasonable job of painting a wall, he was stuck with the moniker.

In his youth he'd been an artist, creative in many ways, writing and playing music, spray painting walls – he could give Banksy a run for his money. His music never made the Top Ten, but always earning enough money for him to lead a comfortable life.

Frankie Bean never stayed in one place very long, he'd loved India, but Thailand had called out to him. Thailand was amazing but he joined a group of travellers back-packing to the Philippines. Sometimes he would forget altogether to keep in touch with his family in Manchester and had missed his sister's wedding, because no one could get in touch to tell him about it.

He had been married briefly but that had not lasted. His lovely wife started hankering to buy a house and start a family. He had to admit that before the wedding he had not protested loudly when she had put forward these ideas, but when it came to the choice he went back to his wanderings.

He had never taken drugs in his younger years, surprising in hindsight, when considering the hippy friends he kept, but for no apparent reason, in his 50s he decided to find out what it was all about. Perhaps it was one of the few experiences he hadn't tried. But it had not been a good experience, his mind and body had reacted to the cocaine, and he had fought for his life for a long time being kept alive in a hospital, until his family had decided to turn off the ventilator. But he hadn't died, just stayed in the coma. It was decided

STORIES

that the best place for him was a care home and he had lived there for 15 years.

The carers were amazing, feeding him, washing him, and keeping him comfortable. As they went about their caring, they chatted to him and gradually he drifted back into consciousness. His speech was the last thing to return but by then he had become institutionalised. The thought of moving out frightened him. To the staff he was Frank the Painter, the lovely polite old man waiting for God, the one who ate everything on his plate and then helped collect the dishes. He helped the home run smoothly by organising card and domino games with the other residents and let them win and the one who occasionally got up to sing on the karaoke and had a half decent voice. But in his mind, Frank was still a young man, striding through rainforests looking for rare flowers, he was singing on a stage in front of crowds of followers or demonstrating outside parliament for equal rights for women or ethnic minorities.

He woke up one morning determined to climb out of his comfort zone and follow his dreams, relive the parts of his youth that he was still capable of. The problem was the inspector, hired by the owner of the home, to cherry pick applications, choosing only the reasonably fit people to become residents. They didn't like people to leave except in a coffin as it didn't look right on reviews. Frank's fees had never faltered for years and more than covered the amount it cost to keep him, bringing a tidy income to the little goldmine of a home.

The inspector had professionals in his pocket, Drs, psychiatrist, social workers who were always willing, for a small back hander to word the reports in the way it suited him. For a year he had been stalling Frank's decision to leave by telling him that he needed permission from the medical professionals. Getting people to talk to him and examine him persuading him that he would not be able to manage on his own. Frank was certain that he was also administering sedatives to keep him docile because sometimes he would look at the calendar and wonder where the past week had gone. He started pretending to swallow the pills and then flushing them away, shamming sleep in the middle of the day until he became clearer headed. But the inspector was too wily, and Frank couldn't find a way to get past him.

Finally, the solution presented itself to him one day as he stared through the windows at the pristine gardens. The next day he put in a request for new furniture for his room. He would of course fund it himself. He told the manager that as he was quite fit and would probably be living here for quite a while, he would prefer the wardrobe and bed to be of his own choosing. The manager and inspector were relieved, at last Frank had given up the idea to leave.

He wrote to one of his old friends and hatched a plan. On the day that the furniture was delivered to his room, he began to rant and rave, a side of Frank that the home had never seen. He shouted and complained that the wardrobe was not good enough quality, and he wanted his money back. The manager apologised to the delivery men, who were surprisingly understanding, and without complaint they willingly and carefully, carried the wardrobe back into the van. He noticed that they seemed to be working up a sweat as they carried it back.

By the time that Frank's disappearance was being investigated, he was in a trendy bedsit in Media City, pouring over plans to see the world. For the price he had been paying for his care home fees, he could join a cruise and travel the world.

STORIES
IBRAHIM
VERONICA SCOTTON

> Wrtiting Challenge: Incorporate the following, in sequence:
> Don't bring that thing into my clean kitchen
> And nobody takes a screwdriver to a disco
> He was so proud of his new skill

Ibrahim did an about turn, he had learned to choose his battles. He'd actually forgotten that he had the bicycle wheel in his hand. His mother's injured voice followed him outside, "And don't leave it where the neighbours can see it, I will never understand why you just don't let Edwin do it, or in fact just buy a new one." Ibrahim smiled, it amused him to think of their gardener/gofer addressed as Edwin, he knew it made Eddy squirm.

He had a vague memory of his father cutting his own lawn, and even topping up the oil in his car, but since becoming a Member of Parliament, his mother had deemed it unseemly for him to undertake these menial tasks.

His grandparents had arrived from New Delhi, in the 60s, Shazia and Mohib met on the ship carrying them to their new lives. They were both six years old and before they landed in Dover their parents had betrothed them. Never having any expectations of being allowed to choose their own spouse, they were happy to celebrate with an extravagant wedding as soon as they had both finished their education. It was a happy and fruitful marriage and their six children, from an early age learned their commandments:

Respect your parents, grandparents and anyone else in authority

Read the Quran every day

Be a straight A student

The two girls and four boys each studied and became doctors, lawyers, or lecturers, and Mohib (named after his father) was the most studious and ambitious, it was no surprise when he became a lawyer and then an MP. He was intelligent and full of energy and shocked his parents by refusing to marry the woman they had chosen for him, a beautiful young cousin who had agreed to give up her life in India to follow the choice of her family. But Mohib had spoken to her by phone and decided that he should give her the chance to marry someone closer to home instead of being shipped abroad. Instead, he had married a beautiful Asian girl whom he had met in college. She was clever and slightly disrespectful and great fun. How could he have known that she would evolve into the snob that she had become? Perhaps it would have been better if they had had more children, but poor Ibbie carried all his mother's ambitions for him on his shoulders.

At the expensive private school where he was boarded, there had been an attempt to make the boys more *rounded,* offering evening and weekend classes in electronics, carpentry and plumbing. His mother gave short shrift to the idea that she would spend good money to allow her son to demean himself by learning a trade. Ibbie got around this by casually mentioning that he was the poorest student in his class "All the other boys have more money to spend at the tuck shop." His allowance was increased immediately, and he paid for his own extracurricular class in electronics.

He needed the bike to visit his fellow pupil and good friend Rupert, who lived in the next village. His parents had equally high hopes for their son, but were under no illusions that they would be unable to keep funding their children's education if their building construction company didn't continue to thrive, and were happy that their son had a plan B. Ibrahim and Rupert became firm friends and enjoyed nothing more than tinkering around with all things mechanical or technical. They also shared a love of cinema and discos. This had been a hard battle to win with his mother. He had refused to do any homework until she agreed to allow him to visit his friend. She wouldn't have minded if he was visiting people from his own class but a common ginger haired white boy? His father stepped in eventually and for once put his foot down, saying that Ibrahim had a right to choose his own friends particularly if they were studying at the same school, and so long as his grades didn't slip.

During the following half term holiday, the boys were looking forward to helping Rupert's dad to put a new engine into one of his trucks. Ibrahim told his mother that he was going to collaborate, with his friend with homework and then go to a disco and would be

STORIES

home late. She insisted that Eddie drive him there and come to pick him up "no later that 10:30". That was an easy compromise, Eddie would never tell tales. As he gave his mother the regulation peck on the cheek, she noticed that he had a screwdriver in his pocket,

"And nobody takes a screwdriver to a disco," she observed."I'm just returning it, it's the one I borrowed to fix my bike"

The friendship continued as did the lessons in electronics. More and more Ibrahim began to dream of having a trade, he didn't want to follow his father into politics or his uncles and aunts into medicine or education. He could relax when he stayed with his friend, he loved to eat his meals around the table with them, he had a crush on Amelia, Rupert's older sister and she teased him about his blushes. But there wasn't a cat in hell's chance that he would be allowed to date a blond, Catholic, older girl.

It was while he was studying at Oxford that the bomb dropped, or bombs. The first one was when his father was sacked from his job and dismissed from parliament, and eventually imprisoned. It had been discovered that he had been spying for the Chinese government. He had also been having an affair with a long-term girlfriend and was up to his eyes in gambling debts, his debtors now clawing them back in. Everything he owned was now mortgaged and he had no idea how he was going to repay. Perhaps he could write a best seller while incarcerated. The second bomb was dropped by his mother, while going apoplectic at her husband's indiscretions (these things could be solved and forgiven, but the public humiliation would never go away). She let slip that her husband had never pleased her sexually and that Edwin's skills didn't end in the garden.

Ibrahim was allowed to finish the term at Oxford and passed with a first. He was welcomed with open arms into his friend's family. The scandal caused by his father would do nothing to propel him into the upper circles and he didn't care. Rupert's dad was reaching retirement age and none of his children, with their expensive education were interested in taking over the business. Ibrahim with his education and love of getting stuck into anything hands on, was the obvious one to take over from him.

He was so proud of his new skill.

THE SYSTEM

Veronica Scotton

> Writing Challenge:
> I had this system for getting exactly what I wanted from people.
> They were all the same I decided.
> The time Lesley called me a leach.

I had this system for getting exactly what I wanted from people. It had been born out of experience when as a toddler, I mastered the tantrum skill, screaming at top pitch until I got the thing I wanted. Afterwards, I would be so exhausted and my throat so sore that I would curl up quietly to recover. Then the discovery, if I stayed quiet long enough, the adults would come to investigate.

"Are you OK darling? Do you want a cuddle?"

Then they would question their earlier decision to allow me to scream.

"What harm is there in letting her eat ice cream at bedtime" or "Perhaps we could just top the bath up with warm water instead of getting her out before she wants to."

I soon skipped the tantrum and went straight to the quiet sulk, the doe eyes, the sighs.

The strategy still worked as I grew through school years. It seems adults begin to worry if their child stops making a noise. I would shrug my shoulders when parents asked me if I had a problem, keeping up the silence for a longer period if the thing I wanted was particularly expensive. When I judged that they were really beginning to worry about me, I would start with short sentences:

"I'm just sad!"

"Why, whatever's the matter sweetheart"

"Everyone in my class has got Ellie Kelly shoes, I'm the only one with Start Right"

"But Start Right are really good for your feet"

"Yes mummy, but It just makes me sad"

STORIES

Then I would revert to the doe eyes, the head resting on one shoulder, the sighs and, with a bit of practice, a tear. That always worked.

Strangely it still worked, when, as an adult, I could manipulate my peers and even employers

They were all the same I decided.

"What's up with you grumpy?"

"Nothing, I'm fine!"

"You don't look fine, are you sickening for something?"

"No, I'm OK"

"Can I get you anything?"

"No thankyou"

"Have I done something to upset you?"

"Not really"

I could keep this up all day, all week or even longer depending on the desired effect. By the time I dropped the charade they would gladly give me the extra day's holiday, lend me their best dress, or go along with my choice of outing, just so long as I reverted to my usual jolly personality.

The only one person who didn't fall for the trick was my older sister Lesley. I knew she had sussed me out the time Lesley called me a leach.

THE BEST BRANDY AND GIN MINCEMEAT EVER

VERONICA SCOTTON

> Inspiration Challenge:
> This was going to be a terrible day
> I thought people only went to Church on Sunday
> The Best Brandy and Gin Mincemeat Ever

It was a bright and sunny day despite it being the middle of winter. But in Jenny's mind, this was going to be a terrible day, one of those days when it's best to stay in bed because everything is going to turn out bad.

It had started off so innocently, well! Perhaps not so innocently! Her friend Craig had bet her that, so long as they were in class for registration, they could slip away, and their absence would not be noticed. He had been correct, during first break they had slipped out of school, through a missing railing and spent the day in Manchester City Centre. Eating a Subway meal was a gastronomic delight compared to school 'puke' and drinking Cola in the sunshine was an improvement on double science.

The good-looking guy with designer jeans and menacing tattoos lounged next to them and thought it hilarious that they were skipping school. He boasted to them that he had hardly had any formal education, he was from a travelling family, his parents thought education after learning to read, write and add up was a waste of time. He entertained them with tales of earning money – cash in hand, "not paying tax to this corrupt government."

As three o'clock came around, the friends began to make a move to return home, The stranger winked at Jenny, "I'm Ian by the way," he gave her his phone number. "Next time you are in Manchester, give us a bell." Flattered that this charismatic man would be interested in her, she boarded the bus with a smile on her face.

Later in the week, Jenny told her friend Izzy about skipping off school with Craig and about the tattooed traveller, she was sceptical, she didn't believe that "Goody Two Shoes" Jenny would have the guts. So, it had to be proved. They found it just as simple to slip

STORIES

away from school again, but the weather was not as good, black clouds were forming as they boarded the bus. Jenny rang Ian's number and he answered immediately. He met the girls as they alighted from the bus just as the rain began to fall "Welcome to summer in Manchester" he quipped. He led them down a side street into a warm stuffy café. He bought them a burger and chips and once again was entertaining, interesting, and flattering. Izzy was hanging onto his every word and Jenny felt justified. She wouldn't be referred to as "Goody Two Shoes" again.

Time flew, and the friends had some lying to do when she arrived home for tea two hours late. She blamed it on Lizzy, saying that she had been feeling ill and she had had to escort her home. She knew that her friend's parents would not dispute this, they were rarely home and when they were, hardly noticed their daughter or her friends. But she felt grown up, Ian had asked the girls to travel to Sheffield with him to meet some friends and hinted that he could show them a way to make some money. How exciting! Perhaps she would be able to buy new trainers instead of waiting until Christmas.

The next week Ian met the girls at the station, looking remorseful. He apologised to them but told them that his mother had taken ill, and he couldn't accompany them on the train but was in a quandary because he had promised a friend that he would drop off a part for a car. The way he worded the question led the girls to believe that it had been their idea to travel to Sheffield and deliver the part. He paid their train fare and gave them £20 each for their trouble. They skipped onto the train with the phone number and address of the friend on Jenny's phone. Looking through the windows as they passed through towns and villages, Izzy saw people turning out of a church and mused "I thought people only went to church on Sundays."

It had all seemed exiting and innocent then! When had she realised that it wasn't?

Wagging off school became a regular occurrence, and their parents had no reason to doubt their words as they met up at the weekend to window shop at the Trafford Centre. Ian introduced them to Vodka.

"It will relax you and no one will smell it on your breath" and then to cannabis "Don't be a baby, everyone does it."

She began to enjoy the light headedness of intoxication and anxious when she couldn't get her "fix."

Ian took away her virginity, telling her she was a beautiful sexy woman. He said he wanted to stay with her forever but needed money in the bank first.

"You are too good to live in a pokey flat, when I've saved enough money for a deposit for a four-bed new build, we will move in together."

Her woolly brain believed him. Izzy was already living with James, the friend in Sheffield. Her parents didn't worry, they had their own lives to live "and Izzy was an adult now, wasn't she?"

Jenny cried when she woke from a drunken sleep to realise that she had been raped.

"How could this have happened"

Why had Ian left her lying vulnerably in a house full of men? But he forgave her for cheating on him. How far had she fallen?

Ian gradually became less loving towards her. He criticised her dress sense and the black circles around her eyes. He quickly became angry when she refused to carry parcels. She had learned that they contained drugs, not car parts. She was in too deep. He threatened her with the police, with her parents and then with violence and death threats. Her weight plummeted; she was no longer the vibrant teenager with the world at her feet.

Her parents knew that she was addicted to drugs and had done everything in their power to persuade her to kick the habit. They couldn't believe their beautiful daughter had fallen so low and asked themselves where they had gone wrong, They were disbelieving and angry. They tried "tough love" locking her in her bedroom, and then bribing her with clothes and holidays, booking her into clinics. But they would never know that if she did as they asked and cleaned up her act as they wanted, they would be made to suffer. If they tried to move away, he would find them, he had family all over the country.

STORIES

Jenny looked back over the last two years and wished she had never skipped school. She wished she was still that precious "Goody Two Shoes".

She was feeling sad. Her whole body was in pain, she needed a fix but had deliberately not taken any drugs. She needed to think this through. She opened the jar of mincemeat and mixed in her whole stash. She had to leave, and she couldn't leave her family behind to suffer.

Her mother would soon enter the kitchen with forced jollity. It was Christmas and she would make her speciality of mince tarts, containing the best Brandy and Gin mincemeat ever. Jenny hoped they would all leave this cruel world together.

CONJOINED TWINS

Veronica Scotton

How different life would be thought Diane if lockdown hadn't happened. She and Mike, her husband of 20 years had always been highflyers. They'd met at a conference, started talking and by the end of the month had moved in together. Both ambitious, she working her way up in the tourist industry, he a builder. They worked hard and long hours and played hard at the weekend. For 2020 they had booked a 3-week safari as a 20th anniversary present to themselves plus a couple of separate holidays with friends.

The only disappointment in their lives had been the inability to have children. After 10 years of trying and three courses of IVF they had finally accepted defeat and were considering adoption. Lockdown had totally changed their day-to-day lives. Instead of getting up at 6 am to shower, dress and apply makeup, before driving to the railway station, Diane had signed in online from her bed at 8.30. At lunchtime she took an hour to tickle around in the garden and signed off at 5.30. Shopping was done online, and she had discovered the enjoyment of cooking from scratch and eating leisurely when Mike came home.

Sometimes they were in bed by 9 o'clock, something that hadn't happened for years except when the day and thermometer had reminded them that her fertility was at its peak. Now the pressure was off, at 45 menopause was on the horizon, sex had nothing to do with making babies. Lounging around in loose comfortable clothes meant that she did not notice the weight that was creeping round her waist, Mike commented that she was becoming more beautiful, her skin and hair were in tip top condition, they put it down to not using straighteners every day and eating healthy food. Only when her sister remarked that she looked blooming in the way some women did in the second trimester, did the suspicion enter her head.

She booked a telephone appointment with her doctor and excitedly told him about the two positive pregnancy results, he asked her when her last period had been and she honestly could not remember as she had stopped waiting for the date to come round

STORIES

each month. An appointment was made for an ultrasound scan at the nearest anti natal clinic. They held hands excitedly as the sonographer squeezed the jelly over her abdomen to help the probe to make good contact with the skin, all their friends and family were on tenterhooks for the news. This was the dating scan, and included a nuchal translucent (NT) scan, offered to older women who are more likely to give birth to a child with Downs Syndrome. The medic had already said she suspected that the pregnancy was quite advanced by the size of the lump.

The happy couple didn't notice at first the worried expression on the sonographer's face and didn't question the reason when she called in a colleague for a second opinion of the image on the screen. The screen was turned around so that the couple could take a first look at their unborn child and asked what they could make out. "Was that two heads? OMG it was twins" Quietly the medic explained that although there was definitely two heads, there appeared to be only one body. She gave them time to think what this meant. Mike let go of his wife's hand as he staggered in shock, the nurse brought him a glass of water, Diane couldn't take in the information and lay stunned.

They drove home in silence, sending the phone calls from the waiting family and friends to message, they should have waited to tell everyone their news until they were sure the news was good. The next morning, they returned to the hospital to speak to a consultant. She explained slowly and kindly that their twin girls' bodies had fused into one, sometime in early pregnancy. She calculated that pregnancy was thought to be about 28 weeks along, but under the circumstances an abortion could still be carried out. She told the couple to go for a walk and discuss their options and then come back and speak to her. They walked in the hospital grounds, and watched other people chatting and laughing together, the sky was blue, "How could the world still be the same when they had just had their dreams shattered so cruelly." Their babies, apart from the conjoining, appeared to be completely intact, all their organs were fully formed, apart from the small size the body was perfect.

What could they do, surely it was cruel to allow these girls to be born alive, but after 10 years of trying, the possibility of a baby with disabilities had been discussed frequently and they had both come to the decision that they would still love it. But this? A girl with two heads, or should it be two girls with a shared body?

In the end the girls made the decision, in the early hours of the next morning, Diane's premature labour started, she was rushed into hospital and the babies were delivered by emergency caesarean section. As they lay in the incubator with the body covered by a tiny blanket, the heads sleeping peacefully, it was easy to fall in love with them. Extremely tiny but perfectly beautiful. They were not expected to live, the consultant explained to the staff that it would be kinder for everyone concerned if the parents were allowed to spend time with their tiny girls until they slipped away. But the girls had other ideas, they didn't die, and the next day Diane expressed colostrum onto a teaspoon and dripped it into their mouths. From the onset it was clear that the girls could not be separated, there was only one set of organs, it was impossible to tell at this point which brain controlled which part of the body.

Three years later as the girls chattered and ran around the house, engulfed in the love of their family they did not question that they were different from other people around. They were just Gracie and Katie, physically identical, personality wise, different as chalk and cheese. Gracie suited her name, she was graceful, she loved having her long blonde hair brushed, she loved all things girly. She didn't talk as much as her twin, but when she did it was well thought out, she was kind and gentle. Katie, loud from the day she was born, yelled for food, for attention, for the sake of being noisy. Her hair at her insistence was short and spikey. Gracie would fall asleep at night while Katie was still demanding "just one more story."

They started school at the local primary, It was a small village school and after the initial inquisitiveness and questions, the other pupils accepted them as they were, as young children do. They were both intelligent, quick learners, learning to read fluently very quickly, but while Grace loved to write stories, Katie found writing boring and would try to distract her sister. She loved to run around kick a ball and climb, being quite fearless. Her sister, the diplomat from the beginning would make a deal. I will play outside at whatever you like, but then you have to do what I want. By the time they had their 7th birthday, Katie had been diagnosed with Dysgraphia which meant that although she could read well and understand what she was reading, she found it difficult to get the answers down on paper. Their teacher was quite OK with Katie telling her sister what to write for her, but later in high school some of her teachers would not be so understanding.

Puberty brought about a change in the girls, Katie, while still a tomboy had become quite studious, Gracie a Goth, dying her hair black and driving the teachers to distraction with her continuous disagreements. In the years since the lock down, Covid had not gone away, but the world had learned to live with it. For reasons not confirmed, all over the world the birthrate had dropped dramatically since 2020. It had been suggested that the young people who had contracted covid, while seemingly unaffected had been rendered infertile. Other scientific experts questioned if it was the vaccine that was causing the infertility it. While it was being investigated, only people past their childbearing age were being offered the vaccine, which had to be administered twice a year. All year 8 children were examined to determine their fertility. The girls learned that they were fine which brought out the angry reaction from Gracie "bloody great, we could have children if some weirdo could be persuaded to fuck the monster" Kate kept her thought to herself, but the thought of bearing a child frightened her, for as long as she could remember she had felt that she had been born into the wrong body. The irony brought a wry smile to her face. Of course, he had been born into the wrong body, his sister's. Kate had felt like a boy all of her life, she would have fought for sex reassignment surgery if she had had her own body, but how could she wish that on her Gracie.

After the Goth episode, Gracie returned to being clothes conscious, their body had bloomed, slim waist, full breasts. Katie still insisted on taking turns as she had in primary school. For each day they dressed in clothes to enhance their figure, a day would be spent in baggy jeans and tee-shirts. For each disco or beauty treatment, there was a football match.

Of course, over the years there had been many scientists that had wanted to use the girls in their dissertations, but the girls' parents had done their best to shield them from the prying eyes, only allowing the doctors and surgeons at their local hospital to conduct tests once a year. It seemed that Gracie, who's head was on the right-hand side, nevertheless controlled the left hand and leg and vice versa. But the girls were so finely tuned to each other that they managed to synchronise their movements, the two hands using a lap top and a piano, their legs running as if only one brain controlled them.

Life carried on; Katie wanted to play women's football at international level but Gracie was not prepared to train for 5 hours each day in order for her sister to reach this level. She wanted to become a pilot and had won a place at uni. This time Katie had to be disappointed, she accompanied her sister to lectures, sometimes tuning out the boring lessons by listening to music through earphones, they did play football very competitively for the local amateur team.

It was during their third year of university lectures that Gracie began to get the headaches and a week after graduation that she had a seizure. They were rushed into hospital where it was discovered the brain tumour in Gracie's brain.

It was suggested that radio therapy could shrink the tumour to a size that could possibly be removed surgically and for a while this seemed to work, but then the tumour began to grow again, surgery was the only option, but it carried the danger of irreparable damage to her brain. The twins discussed the problem, as it of course involved both of them. Should they take the chance with surgery or live their life to the full for as long as they had left. Gracie in the end had to be the one to make the decision, sadly after all her hard work it seemed that she would never get to become a pilot, she should have let Katie take a shot of being a footballer.

The surgery was planned, the girls wrote their wills. Gracie bequeathed her share of her body to Katie, making her promise that if she died, then her sister would live life to the full in her memory. They wrote letters to all their friends and family thanking them for their love that had brought the girls happiness for the last 20 years. Their parents threw an early 21st party and they had a family holiday and planned their funeral. It was presumed that if Gracie died in surgery, then Katie would also die.

STORIES

The tumour was removed successfully, but then Gracie's brain suffered an aneurism and died. For the second time in their lives, the twins were expected to die. Katie, woke up after surgery and along with everyone else expected to follow her sister into the next world. And for the second time, that didn't happen. In the beginning, Katie couldn't use her right arm or leg and so found it impossible to walk and even difficult to sit unaided, but a miracle happened, gradually her brain took over the electronic impulses that were no longer coming from her sister's lifeless brain so that she could learn to walk again. Their heart still pumped blood around the body and up into Gracie's brain so that the cheek that touched Katie's cheek didn't deteriorate. She felt like she had done, all those years ago, when Grace would fall asleep, and she would be awake and listening to one more story. It was their parent's will that Gracie's lifeless head be removed and laid to rest. This was very difficult for Kate to agree to. Her sister had been a part of her since the womb, where did Katie end and Gracie begin? She decided that she would fulfil Gracie's dream and become a pilot, she had learnt quite a lot of the material while joining Gracie during the lectures in uni. And unbelievably she found that when using her left hand, Gracie's hand, her Dysgraphia disappeared.

Within the year she had completed her degree and received a diploma and 5 years later was flying commercial planes. Her ambition to play football slipped away as did the idea of sex reassignment. She introduced herself to new people as Gracie and in time became a wife and mother.

INNOCENCE LOST

COLIN BALMER

> Writing Challenge:
> An interesting experience

Alan and Julie got down from the early evening train at Blackpool Central on a darkening October night. The train had been packed with city folk out to 'see the lights', but the teenagers were not on an illuminations mission. He carried all he needed in a duffle bag: she in a copious holdall. There was a rank of five or six black cabs waiting for the innocents. They got in the first.

"C-c-can you find us a B and B for the night," Alan stammered embarrassed. "How much is it?"

"Sure thing. Boss," the driver replied and pulled off the station. "Pay me when we get there."

Alan turned and smiled to Julie, "You know, I think this is the first time I've been in a taxi. It's the first time I've paid anyway."

"Yes," she agreed, "Me, too. Taxi! You know how to treat a girl, don't you? We go everywhere by bus from the estate. Town, hospital, work. Only one or two buses. Never any need for taxi."

"Of course. Even when I go clubbing with the lads, we can always get the late-night bus and walk the last mile or so. You should see some of the drunks that get on. I think my dad got us in a taxi once on holiday, but it might have been one of his mates."

After ten minutes around the streets of the resort and a look at the lights, the cab pulled up in a back street where it seemed every one of the Victorian four-floor houses was offering B&B.

"Here we are, Boss. Tell Mrs McCall that Jim Kelly brought you and you'll be well looked after and," with a wink to Alan, whispered, "she's discreet."

"What's the damage?" Alan remembered hearing his dad asks the same, bringing his mam home from a family wedding, Belle Vue dogs or another special occasion.

"Just seven bob, boss."

STORIES

Alan handed over a ten shilling note and a half crown, "Keep the change" he declared loudly enough for his girlfriend to hear and be impressed by his magnanimous generosity.

He thought *Smith* would have been too obvious, so signed in to Mrs McCall's Dunroamin as *Mr and Mrs G Best*, the first name that came to a mind full of Saturday's game against Liverpool. Mrs McCall handed over their room key and cautioned that the front door will be locked at midnight sharp and 'no noise after 11pm.' Neither of the youngsters had any intention of drawing attention to their clandestine coalition.

They dropped their bags in the 'double room with sea view,' located the bathroom six doors down the corridor and went out. Neither had eaten. After rushing home from work, quickly getting changed and packed, they had caught the bus to Piccadilly for the evening train and the trip to the seaside. It had taken his breath away on Tuesday when she suggested that 'now is the time.' He'd been a trembling cauldron of nerves until Friday came and glorious inevitability assuaged any terror.

Exhibiting commendable self-control, Alan and Julie, took to the streets of Blackpool and enjoyed fish and chips in a tram shelter, before a gentle saunter through the famous illuminations. They dropped into a pub next to the train station, had a pint of mild and Cherry B and left with the sound 'the turn' in their ears at half past ten. They could still hear the singer as they rounded a corner and spotted their digs a short stride away.

"We could have walked it from the station," said Julie, stepping through the front door.

"Well, I won't get screwed by the next taxi driver. Chalk it up as a new experience. Now…"

FRANK THE PAINTER

COLIN BALMER

Writing Challenge:	
Protagonist: Frank the Painter	His Aim: To be Wild and Free
Obstacle: The Inspector	Action: Buys a new wardrobe

The idea first occurred to Frank McTavish as he looked down from his perch 360 foot above the Firth of Forth. The magnificent panorama from here had been exciting thirty-four years ago when he joined the maintenance gang as apprentice painter. Now foreman, he smiled, recalling the first job that apprentices were given was to 'just paint the rivets until you master your craft' - it was estimated that the bridge contained something like seven million. Frank had soon found out that the red oxide paint, known as 'Forth Bridge Red', was the same for the whole steel structure nearly two and a half miles long and rivets were not given individual attention. He wanted to get away from the repetitive task of painting this bridge. No sooner finished at the North Queensferry end than they had to start again on the Edinburgh side. Painting the red bridge had accounted for all his working life and, as he approached his half century on the planet, he wanted to leave his personal *rock of Sisyphus* to be wild and free – to see more of the world and experience unimagined pleasures.

'Once the girders in this pier are finished,' he told himself, 'I will make my suggestion to Network Rail and everybody can have a break.'

But he had McNair, the structural inspector to by-pass first. He preciously guarded all lines of communication with the bridge management and owners. In the past, whenever Frank had wanted to talk to someone higher up, McNair had insisted he put it in writing and he himself would see it was passed on. Strangely nothing ever came of the painter's suggestions.

Ernie, Frank's younger brother, was a maintenance engineer on a North Sea oil rig – making a small fortune in the process. During one of their late-night pub sessions, they had compared paintwork on the rigs with that on Frank's bridge. Surely the technology must

STORIES

be transferable? Frank had spent weeks writing up a plan from stripping the 120 years of paint layers back, sand blasting bare metal and applying a glass flake epoxy paint. It would be necessary to shield the work from the environment and even hand paint where the spray guns could not reach. A massive undertaking in itself, but McNair would stop the plan getting off the ground.

Another alcoholic indulgence put a plan in Frank's mind. On a weekend in July with pleasant weather, he went to the local IKEA in Edinburgh and invested in a Kleppstad double door wardrobe. Before his shift started on Monday, he took the flat-pack and assembled it against the pillar he was working on. He drew from the plentiful supply of red paint and blended the wardrobe into the bridge structure and waited for McNair's morning inspection round.

'Mr McNair, could you come and check this latest batch of paint?' he asked.

'Aye, laddie,' a patronising response to the middle-aged artisan came from the inspector.

'Just here in the paint locker.'

McNair stepped into the wardrobe.

'I canna see anything,' was the last he said before the door slammed shut and Frank turned the key.

He was still shouting and banging inside the red IKEA box as it floated out on the tide into the North Sea

'The McTavish Plan' as it became known was accepted by the board after six months deliberation and the ten year project was competed in 2011 at a cost of £30 million – the original bridge had cost only £3million to build in 1889 and taken six years. It was not expected that the bridge would need repainting for twenty years.

'Wild' Frank McTavish, former bridge painter, was last heard of bungee jumping off a bridge in New Zealand to celebrate his fiftieth birthday spending his employee incentive bonus. Masters on ocean-going vessels entering the Firth of Forth are careful to avoid a new shipping hazard which looks like a red rectangular buoy.

*Sisyphus was condemned by the gods to push a rock up the hill but it kept rolling back down again.

SUE FINDS LOVE.

COLIN BALMER

Writing Challenge:	
Protagonist: Sue, who reviews books	Her Aim: to find true love
The obstacle: m the woman in 3B	Solution: learns to foresee the future

When Sue first came to us, she appeared to be the ideal complement to our group's capabilities. Swinton creative writing group SWit'CH have skilful English writers and grammarians to give us the assurance that we can meet our quality criteria. Keen readers of a medley of genres, with disparate life experiences and interests, we have at our command a large lexicon and extensive vocabulary to make our creations original and interesting. We have, over time, developed technology skills and advanced into self-publishing of our works. When Sue applied to join the writing group she brought with her a career as book reviewer and gave us another string to the SWit'CH bow.

Forlorn at first, she admitted that she had probably been too singularly focused on her publishing house's specialisation. Mills & Boon as a genre had limited her outlook and brainwashed her into the belief that true love was all that mattered in life. But, sadly, our heroine bookworm, reading in her lonely apartment, had never come across the dashing masculine paradigm the novels invariably anticipated. She confessed that her ideal partner could have been the civil airline pilot, Jarvis McCool, whom she passed in the corridor on his way to her neighbour in apartment 3B. The red light over the door of 3B would be dimmed during his overnight visits, but her restricted subject material with Mills & Boon did not explain the situation behind the closed door.

Lonely Sue resolved her frustration, however, after sharing the lift with the lady from 3B. Weighing her up 'in the cold light of day', Sue saw a rapidly ageing, world-worn, fallen beauty.

"I foresee no long-term future there." She told herself. "Powder, paint and synthetic structural support will only help so far. That old tart will be worn out soon, so I can move in."

STORIES

For three weeks she stalked Jarvis and 3B, making notes on the face she had 'slapped on' (by the bucket-load) to fill the cracks, her dress styles and hair extensions and wigs appropriate to each occasion. She recorded the occasions when Jarvis would smile longingly, what upset him, where they would go whenever they ventured away from flat 3B.

When Jarvis appeared in the corridor that November evening, luscious Sue was ready. Charismatically coiffured, cosmetically complemented and dressed impeccably she closed the door to her apartment and walked toward 3B in the fashion, to which its resident had aspired. She had spotted the desirable aviator entering the building and co-ordinated their meeting as he came out of the lift.

"Oh, sir. I am so sorry to have to tell you that your friend in 3B has been rushed away to some hospital by ambulance. I heard the first responder muttering something about 'early onset dementia' and having her taken in 'for her own good'."

Smiling her most beguiling, she sympathised, "I'm sure you will be saddened but, if it's any consolation, you could come to my little apartment and I will comfort you!"

Members of SWit'CH are looking forward to reading, with lascivious longing, her published revelations about her new career.

PLAGUE IN THE VILLAGE

Caroline Barden

It had been a hot summer's day without a breath of wind, setting the perfect scene for the village's midsummer fair. People were strolling down the street towards the evening entertainment or sitting somnolently on the roadside benches licking ice creams.

Ben waited drowsily in the kitchen for Jenny to finish her work, feeling too lethargic to hurry her up.

"Is this it?" Jenny murmured to herself, running her finger over an image on the computer screen, her heart banging with anticipation. She left a smear of sweat on the glass as she traced the roofline of the church and circled the black figure in the foreground, the distinctive long-beaked mask of the plague doctor clearly in view.

"Ben, come and see," she called. "I think I've found the picture I need." She heard him sigh as he scraped his chair back on the quarry tiles of the kitchen floor, but he came through to look. He peered at the grainy picture.

"It could be, I suppose," he said. "The church looks about right but I'm not sure about the lychgate though … and is that our cottage? It looks a bit different somehow."

Tears of frustration glistened in Jenny's eyes: she had scrutinised innumerable ghastly images relating to the plague, searching for any old drawings or prints that connected her village and the disease.

"Leave it now, Jenny," Ben said, putting his arm around her. "Let's go to the village fair. Take your mind off this disgusting disease."

"Not yet." There was a tremor in Jenny's voice. "You go. I'll catch you up."

Ben slammed the front door as he went, and a hush enveloped the ancient cottage.

Jenny lifted her fair hair off her damp neck, scrunching it up with a pencil, and settled down to scrolling through the grim images. She mulled over the comments her editor at the magazine had made when he'd rejected her last article as being too dull.

"Evidence, Jenny," he'd said, tearing at his hair. "Evidence, that's how you bring it to life."

She was sure he really wanted to keep her on, even though he hadn't printed anything of hers for several weeks, but this was her last chance to bring him something intriguing. She knew the readers loved to read about gruesome events in history, especially if it related to their own area, so she'd chosen to investigate what happened in their village during the plague, particularly thinking about the neglected area in the graveyard over their garden wall that really might be a plague pit as some of the older villagers said.

It wasn't long before Jenny eye's felt heavy with sleep. "Just a few more minutes," she said to herself, "and then I'll go and find Ben at the fair."

Something crashed in the kitchen and Jenny jerked with surprise, her skin prickling in the heat. "That cat, again," she said to herself as she went to see.

Broken glass and dried herbs littered the floor where a jar had fallen. A sickly-sweet smell of pounded leaves – lavender, sage and rosemary – drifted in the stifling air. The herb-stuffed beak of the plague doctor came to Jenny's mind, and she shivered as an icy chill trickled down her back. She stepped outside into the sunlight. All was still and silent, not a cat to be seen.

Glancing beyond the garden wall Jenny scanned the church and lychgate wondering if the differences in the picture she had found were just artistic licence. In the orange rays of the setting sun the boughs of a yew tree cast deep shadows over the churchyard. Something moved in the gloom. Slowly, slowly, a figure emerged into the brightness – sunlight splintering around the form. It was a man, his long hair and beard wild-looking around his face and his dark clothes ragged. He was doubled up, clutching his stomach, shuffling. He leant heavily on a gravestone. When he turned and saw Jenny, he cried out, in a voice so quiet that she could hardly hear, "Help me, please."

The man's haggard face was visible now and the livid, suppurating sores reminded Jenny of the images on her computer.

No one else was there. Jenny's breath caught in her throat and a feeling of nausea rose up. She looked hopelessly at the wall, she couldn't climb it, she would have to go around. Her legs felt stiff and heavy.

"I'll call an ambulance," she shouted. "Hold on."

Darkness fell suddenly as Jenny stumbled back inside. She reached out for the light-switch, but the lights were dead.

"Keep calm," Jenny told herself, her breath fast and shallow, but the cloying smell of herbs had been joined by a noxious smell of burning and she felt light-headed and dizzy. In the pitch black she searched in vain for her phone. Nothing was in the right place.

"Ben, I need you." A forlorn whisper that Jenny knew he couldn't hear.

She knocked a chair over, and as the clatter died away she heard strange sounds through the open windows. The rhythmic clanging of a handbell which echoed in the chimney.

A woman weeping, long, drawn-out wails of desolation. Horses' hooves on the cobbles in the front lane with a rumbling of cartwheels. The floor shook gently, and Jenny closed her eyes against the blackness.

Stumbling forward with her arms outstretched Jenny made for the front door her mind full of the computer images of the plague. After what seemed to an eternity, she found the door latch and she breathed a sigh of relief. But it seemed stuck. She pulled and wrenched at the door, desperate now to get out, and eventually was able to open it up. But inside the doorway a wall blocked her way. Jenny's legs turned to jelly and with cobwebs tangling into her hair she sank down to the floor. "Ben, where are you?" she whispered as she rested her head on her knees.

A short while later, Ben opened the front door and snapped on the light. "I'm home, Jenny," he yelled, wondering why she was in the dark. Then he noticed the disarray in the room and saw Jenny crouching on the floor in an alcove he had never seen before. In no time he had his arms around her and, listening to her fantastical tale, he helped her brush off the dust and cobwebs. She persuaded him to take a torch and search the graveyard for the sick man, but he could not find anyone.

As Ben swung the torch around on his way back into the cottage something caught his eye.

"I think that dusty alcove must have been the original front door," he said, "and look at what I've found on the floor."

He handed Jenny an old ledger, its cover dry and flaky.

Jenny opened the book carefully and gasped at its contents, feeling faint and dizzy at the awfulness of her evening and the enormity of her find. "I think it's all the evidence I need, Ben. A record of all the people who died in the plague," she cried.

SEEDS was written in 2003, to highlight the futility of war. However, it is an unfortunate and uncomfortable truth that some wars are necessary, otherwise ---- we would all have been under the German 'jackboot'.

POEMS & A PLAY

SEEDS.

The seeds of war are scattered,
by our leaders' hand.
The seeds of war are sown,
in some foreign land.

Is it hate? Is it greed?
Or just your vanity?
Is this your reason,
for such inhumanity?

Where is your guilt,
as you maim, kill and destroy?
Are you the one who steals,
the man ---- from the boy?

Why should we follow,
blindly, like lost sheep?
Believing all your promises,
we know you'll never keep.

Why should we listen,
to all that you incite.
We would rather live in peace
a basic ---- human right.

The seeds of war are scattered
by our leaders' hand.
The seeds of war are gathered,
in some ---- foreign land.

WARREN DAVIES

Fear was written in 2004.

Fear is an ambivalent emotion. Is it friend, or foe?
Too much fear can immobilise us. Too little fear can imperil us. I suppose we all have to find our personal threshold on how much fear is......fearsome.

POEMS & A PLAY
FEAR

Are you afraid of your past,
the mistakes you made that seem to last.

Are you afraid of growing old,
frail and weak when nights turn cold.

Are you afraid of the unknown,
do you reap what you have sown?

Are you afraid of being poor,
if your children ask for more.

Are you afraid of the truth,
even if you have the proof.

Are you afraid of walking tall,
would you rather creep and crawl.

Are you afraid of love's pain,
is your loss someone's gain.

Are you afraid of your fear,
this friend or foe is always near.

WARREN DAVIES

This poem was written in 2014.
It was originally going to be titled: STOLEN. However, I decided to settle for the unambiguous title of: DEMENTIA.
In 2011, my wonderful mother, Ann, was diagnosed with this cruel and callous illness. It was the start of a long slow slide into.....oblivion. Dementia had insatiably, and insidiously, stolen Mam's cognitive capacity, mobility, independence and dignity. It had also stolen her from me. Mam died with dementia 16 Jan 2017.
I can only offer my sincerest sympathy to the sufferer, and trust they will be well cared for with compassion, love, and understanding.

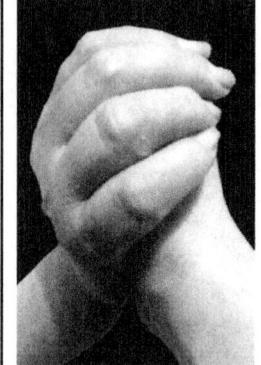

POEMS & A PLAY
DEMENTIA (SLIDING AND SLIPPING)

Sliding:
Into the darkest deepest
depths of despair
Slipping
like an old coin
down the back of a chair.

Silently: hoping someone is there,
Silently: praying someone will care.

Looking not seeing
Listening not hearing
Touching not feeling
Breathing not living

The sun never shines
the clouds never drift
the rain never stops
the fog never lifts.

How dark is this room?
How deep is this hole?
Stealthily stealing
mind, body and soul.

WARREN DAVIES

It would appear that the cult of 'Health and Safety' has permeated every State organisation in the country. Paradoxically, so called H & S rules and regulations can – be prejudicial to a persons health and safety. It cannot be denied, that there have been tragic consequences from health and safety directives: either because of callow incompetence, or, callous indifference. " Safety-First" and "Risk-Assessment" have become euphemisms for 'doing-nothing'. How far will this mission-creep travel?When will common sense return? Or, is that too risky? Harsh? Yes. Accurate? Probably. If we want to stay safe; perhaps we should all stay in bed: then again, the bed might collapse.

POEMS & A PLAY

HEALTH AND SAFETY

I-dotting
T-crossing
Box-ticking
Mouse-clicking
Pen-pushing
Paper-shuffling
Form-filling
Rubber-stamping
Red-taping
Rule-making
Regulating
Spirit-sapping
Soul-stripping
Status-quoing
Quango-cratting
Fence-sitting
Hair-splitting
Finger-wagging
Buck-passing
Clip-boarding
Hard hat-wearing
Jack-booting
Goose-stepping
Muscle-flexing
Margin-measuring
Risk-assessing
Life-threatening.

WARREN DAVIES

How many billions?

POEMS & A PLAY

THE COMMITTEE (HS2)

The committee, after much:

Head scratching,
Hair curling,
Eyebrow raising,
Nose picking,
Lip pursing,
Teeth grinding,
Throat clearing,
Jaw dropping,
Chin stroking,
Shoulder shrugging,
Hand wringing,
Thumb twiddling,
Nail biting,
Navel gazing,
Buttock clenching,
Bollock scratching,
Knee bending,
Feet shuffling,
Toe curling,
and
Soul searching.
Have concluded that we haven't
got, a f..king clue:
what to do with...HS2.

WARREN DAVIES

This poem was written in 1982; when we had 'tramps' or, 'gentlemen' of the road – before begging and homelessness became an epidemic.
I was intrigued by how they had arrived at this stage in their life. What was the catalyst? A broken marriage? A loss of job? Had society turned its back on them or, had they turned their backs on society?
Who knows? What we do know is that: everyone of us is vulnerable to the 'hard-knocks' of life. Forty-years later, we are still asking the same questions.

POEMS & A PLAY
A FORGOTTEN MAN

Dishevelled and derelict
a man walks alone;
Aimlessly drifting
chilled to the bone.
Through hostile winds
and angry rain;
In search of solace
to ease the pain.
A forgotten man
A forgotten past;
forlorn and friendless
a man without caste.
Starved of pity
stripped of pride;
a long time ago
his dignity died.
In a shop doorway
a bed for a night;
swathed in newspaper
under a bright neon light
Scavenging and scrounging
streets without hope;
Sliding further and further
down life's slippery slope.
So! Who is this man?
And, do we care?
Probably not!
But we stand and stare.
For a life on the streets
there are thousands the same;
and if this is so, then -
who is to blame?

WARREN DAVIES

Time
Written in 2004.
Time will always irrepressibly, and irreversibly, march on :with or without us. I once read that time is the universal currency we all share; and that we are born with only so uch to spend, and – nobody ever knows the exact amount. Unfortunately, we are all guilty of wasting and taking for granted this precious commodity-until it runs out.

POEMS & A PLAY

TIME

A clock ticks
a heart beats;
a tap drips
the past retreats.
Still!
Time will not wait
it keeps marching on;
echoing the lives
of everyone.
Second by second
day by day;
the present, like cobwebs
is swept away.
Still!
Time will not wait
it keeps marching on;
with a silent salute
for what's been and gone.
Month after month
year after year;
the seasons unfold
a future unclear.
Still!
Time will not wait
it keeps marching on;
through wind and rain
through mist and sun.
Marching ticking
beating dripping;
on and on
on and on.
Time! will not wait;
for anyone.

WARREN DAVIES

This poem was written to commemorate seventy-five -years of the holocaust. It will, forever, be an indelible stain on the 'soul' of humanity – we must never ever forget. Truthfully, can we ever be certain this industrial mass murder, will never be repeated? Haven't we already witnessed genocides in Bosnia, Darfur, and Rwanda?

POEMS & A PLAY

THE TRAIN

*The train trembles
hissing to a halt;
Freighted with fear
sealed in a vault.
The cold air chills
the sliding bolt.*

*Through iron gates
behind barbed wire;
Flames of flesh
grow higher and higher;
Choose your prayer
but not --- your pyre.*

*Stand to the left
stand to the right;
Too scared to speak
too frail to fight;
Cruelly clothed in ---
blue and white.*

*Old and sick
Slav, Gypsy, Jew;
Husband, wife
and children too;
Stripped and starved
which one were you?*

*Where did you stand
in the queue ?*

WARREN DAVIES

POPPIES

Remembrance – why?
I wrote the poem for our writing group on the subject of poppies. The last line is the focus of this blog. Why? This year's Remembrance service at the Royal Albert Hall focused not only on the first Great War and WW2, but on subsequent wars, including Korea. My key question is why do world leaders go to war? Why, after all these years, have lessons not been learned? In the context of the current wars in Ukraine and Gaza, war and death is once more a feature of our sad and troubled world. Will it never end?
I am reading a Ken Follett novel, based on historical facts, that features through the eyes of its characters, the chilling tensions between America, Berlin and Russia during the Cold War, and how close the world came to annihilation in the sixties by nuclear bombing. The reason – communism versus capitalism. Why? Was it fear? Why should differing ideologies provoke hatred and mistrust amongst humanity? Where does negotiation and communication fit with the need to deal with difference?
What part does religion play in war? Does it really matter what people believe, or whether they worship as Christians, Muslims, Sikhs, Jews, or any other version of religion? It shouldn't! Beliefs are surely personal and private to each individual. Why do we attack others who do not worship in the same way?
So the final line of my poem, asks why our annual remembrance cannot bring lasting peace across the world? Of course, there is no answer to this. I am naive. But let's consider what it means to be human. Through our language and use of words we have the capacity for reasoning, emotion and love. How different are we to the animals from which we have evolved? Animals fight over their territories, or for power over particular animal groups? They fight through necessity – for survival mainly. Can that be said about warring humans? Do world leaders really wage war merely to survive? Neither ideology, nor power, nor religion can ever be valid reasons to kill.
So, one question invites another – why has remembrance not brought everlasting peace – and are some humans really much different from the animals we have all descended from?
War is beyond animal behaviour!

SYLVIA EDWARDS

POEMS & A PLAY

Lonely poppies grow in empty fields
Reminding us, lest we forget,

That war is never far removed from peace,
Lies too often lurk beneath the truth,
Love, once lost, is soon transformed to hate,
And surface beauty often masks the ugly.

Across those fields where blood did soak the earth,
And death brought silence to the land,
Poppies raised their petals to the sun
As souls of dead men, dancing round their graves.

Poppies waving in a gentle breeze,
Reminding us, lest we forget,

That life is never far away from death,
And, like the blood-red petals of the flower,
Can be crushed in the blinking of an eye,
By men at war, forced to forget that they are human.

Now ....years later

Fresh, young blood seeps into hard ground
Where buildings once stood proud and tall – now rubble,
Blood not of soldiers, but of crying children,
Tears and wailing echo forth the age-old question – why?

Petals flutter onto shoulders, as silent symbols of hope,
Still reminding us, lest we forget,

That remembrance alone has not yet brought
Everlasting peace.

WHERE NO BIRDS SING

From life to death
A poem I wrote in 2018 was inspired by the film 'Journey's end', featuring the last moments of soldiers in WW1 trenches. Notice the lines of verse (6..5..4..3..2.....1): counting down to their last breaths. The film greatly affected me emotionally, but my poem also emulated the social class differences, still acted out to the end – though death was imminent (verses two and three).

When we die we all leave this world in the same way: we simply take our final breath. Our hearts stop beating. It is of little consequence or significance whether we are monarchy, lords, rich or poor, old or young, beautiful or ugly. Nor does death measure whether a person has been kind or cruel, good or bad, clever or with special needs. In death race fades into oblivion. All souls are the same colour – if they are any colour at all. It seems to me that once death takes us, every mind and every body becomes exactly the same. We are as dead leaves, fallen from the great tree of life!

So my question is why, throughout life, do humans strive to be so different? Or indeed, why does difference cause such tension and animosity? As we struggle with the challenges of living, why does competition often smother cooperation? In 1914, those chains of social class still hung as yokes around necks, carried from long established tradition, when imagined differences between aristocracy and working class were thought to be important – even during war, as the grim reaper hovered. But are they still? Was not privilege merely an accident of birth: one that enabled greater chances in life? How far have we come towards so-called levelling up: allowing opportunities for those not born into the privileged class to climb the social ladder and improve their lives?

My real point: does it matter which social class we inhabit during life? A resounding NO! Is the King (with his capital letter) more important than any of us? No. So let's all be proud of who we are, whatever colour of skin we have, whatever brain power we have or whatever we have achieved in life. It's not the end that matters, but the process of reaching it.

Do I believe in the soul? I am reserving judgement until my final moment. I will know when I need to know. But, in my imagined afterlife, I visualise a space into which we all pass through. In this space, candles, as eternal souls, glow in the darkness, casting shadows. Each candle is exactly the same size and shape, cylindrical, unadorned. Each burns at the same rate and casts the same intensity of light and shadow around this community of common, human souls. The candle wax never burns down, but remains constant. Do these souls communicate? Yes. Each flicker of candlelight carries meaning, contributing to the communal afterlife – in a silent place where all souls are the same.

A final thought, as you read my poem: the trains carrying all our souls to their final resting place do not have first and second class carriages.

SYLVIA EDWARDS

POEMS & A PLAY

Stinking of shit, they stand strong in ankle-high mud,
In trenches, leaning against rotting wood, rusty metal.
Stare, unseeing, across that charred and blackened place
A land once blessed with colour and nature's bounty,
Before men had made it a space of still silence
Bleached greyness, trees stripped of seasons, where no birds sing.

They wait!

Dinner at eight! In the officers' dug out, wine,
In fine, cut glass goblets – each hand raised to a toast.
Soup made with water, and little else. 'Pass the pepper.'
Cutlets, of something. Nobody asks. Three apricots,
Out of a tin, scraped up with spoons, from metal plates.

They wait!

Their men eat up top, hunched on a bench, dunk dry bread,
In weak tea, laugh, talk of home – as smiles mask their fear.
At this last supper, men with nothing in common
But hope, pen letters to loved ones so far away.

And wait!

The shells drop with an ear-splitting boom! Smoke! Choking!
Silence! All breaths extinguished. Neither stench, nor mud,
Nor rain, nor sun will bother them. Their time has come.

But wait!

Their journey's end? Listen! Wind gently whispers, hums,
A hymn – accompanying souls to eternity.

They're gone.

Nothing moves. Naked waste – lifeless as the moon, where,

No birds sing

ODE TO LIFE, POSITIVITY AND WRITING

Your Journey – Your Way

Life is a journey. We surely agree, though our respective journeys follow varied pathways. Whether long or short, smooth or bumpy, your journey should always represent and characterise YOU. Our journeys help us to find and understand ourselves. I have just completed my memoirs, and I hope they represent my personal journey – travelled my way.

From when I first 'discovered' its self-healing powers, writing has led my journey: and saved me from myself: a strong assertion. From being a highly sensitive and under-confident teenager – then through love relationships that brought their share of challenges, my story, like that of many others, has been one of intense drama, throughout which I have often felt myself drowning between a split personality. My memoirs are written from the perspective of four roles that have characterised ME: woman, teacher, writer and mother/grandmother.

So, my writing journey? My first piece was an article on depression, published (1988) in the 'Christian Herald' magazine. From that moment, as I translated dark thoughts and emotions into written words, opening my heart as I did so, writing has become my leading role on a stage where we are all, as Shakespeare asserted, mere players. I wrote from the heart.

My teacher role inspired me to write fourteen books (published by Routledge) for school staff, plus a further five for parents, about how education could be improved for children with SEND. I also drafted a novel (finally published 2023), as well as articles, short stories and poems, some of which saw publication in magazines. Two recent books, one a whimsical reflection on issues I care about (2021), and a historical novel (2023), now float aimlessly around in the huge sea of Amazon self-publications.

So, writing has helped me to finally triumph over the challenges and stumbling blocks along my pathway, and propped up my other roles: having shone a lit candle into personal periods of darkness.

Writing, at its creative best, also has the potential power to create meaningful triangular connections – linking writer, message and reader. Writers need to be readers. Writing and reading support each other.

Your journey – your way. Do these words reflect inner and outer selves: being happy and confident in our own skins, having the courage to express our thoughts according to personal values and never deviating from what we each regard as 'goodness'? Writing, heart-felt, has characterised my journey. The poem emulates these reflections.

POEMS & A PLAY

Life's too short, no time to waste,
Seize your moments with great haste.
Seek the best from every day,
Find your gold beneath the grey.
Glimpse that nugget, gently shining,
Inside your cloud's silver lining.

See it, smell it,
Taste and touch it.
Your senses wired,
To be inspired!

From that purpose deep inside,
Cultivate your sense of pride.
Make, create, invent and do,
Paint on your skin that inner you.
From the elf upon the shelf,
Steal some magic for yourself.

Then, as you WRITE,
Your soul takes flight,
Your spirit feeds,
And your heart bleeds.

SYLVIA EDWARDS

The **Guinea Pig Club**, established in 1941, was a social club and mutual support network for British and allied aircrew injured during World War II. Its membership was made up of patients of Archibald McIndoe in Ward III at Queen Victoria Hospital, East Grinstead, Sussex, who had undergone experimental reconstructive plastic surgery, including facial reconstruction, generally after receiving burns injuries in aircraft. The club remained active after the end of the war, and its annual reunion meetings continued until 2007.

POEMS & A PLAY
MY 'GO TO' FRIEND

I have a 'go to' friend, I met him years ago
Although we're very different, he always seems to know
The way I think, the way I feel, connected at the core
We see each other rarely, when I need him he'll open up the door

He has seen the world, in a way I'll never know
He has been to places, I would not wish to go
For he has served his country, for eighty years or more
And the stories of his past he holds in his great store

He has a sense of humour, as black as black can be
And sometimes I've been lucky and he's shared his sense with me
His friends have told their stories, allowed me to share with them
I count myself as lucky, to have known McIndoe's men

They flew their planes with gusto, up into the far blue skies
And then came back to earth with lifelong strengthened ties
But now there are not many of these most precious men
But my 'go to' friend will say he's "just another one of them"

CHRISTINE BARWOOD

LITTLE RED POPPY

Up and over,
Out of the trench,
Into the battlefield.
It's raining,
And I'm absolutely drenched.

Cannons roar. Guns fire.
Today. Lost a few troops,
Wondering if it's all worth it.
Fighting for Peace.

When we get back home,
The only memory is a poppy
To symbolise the dead.
Oh, Little poppy – little and red.

PAUL HALLOWS.

POEMS & A PLAY

I'M LONELY

Now I'm a widow, folk so kind
Lovingly keeping me in mind
AH I'm lonely.

Places to go, people to see
Keeping myself very busy
BUT I'm lonely

Back at my hobby pursuits
With new ones to boot
FOR I'm lonely

Grandkids of who boast
As kith & kin I oft host
YET I'm lonely

With no husband to blame
Life's now not the same
SO I'm lonely

We shared many a year
Both grew grey hair
OH I'm lonely

ROSEMARY SWIFT

ODE TO OSTRICHISM

(Burying Our Heads in the Sand)

David Beckham a hero?
God, how we've lost the plot
The real world is filled with heroes
Who'll no more see the light of day
For yesterday's heroes are all dead and gone
Lost in battle
Somewhere!
Didn't make it home
From the bloody war
Seventeen, eighteen
No age at all to die
Such undignified death
Under an alien sky
Fathers, sons, brothers
Gone in the twinkling of an eye
Because some half-crazed bureaucrat
Wants a finger in every pie
Surely we can't believe that war
Can ever lead to peace, but
It's not on our doorstep

POEMS & A PLAY

So we can pretend at least
That it's not happening
It's just a film shown on TV
We've become desensitised
Not knowing truth
From reality

Terminator, Spiderman, Superman
Live to fight another day
After being blown to kingdom come
But it's only make-believe, hey?
Isn't it?

But somewhere, someone lost
A husband, father, son
It's all too real for them
They can't switch it off and on.

MARY YOUNG

OLD AGE

Don't get old
That's what they say
Just stay young
and be on your way.
Your back will ache
Pain to bear
Your knees will knock
Wear and tear
You may get falsh teeth
That lie at your bedside
You start to forget some things
Where's the TV remote
Where are your keys
You find them in strange places
Like in the fridge
Or somewhere else
Sometimes old age
Is not so bad
Lots of fun times
To be had
On holidays and trips out you go
Maybe to a stage show
Some people look at old age oh so bleak
On your Zimmer frame looking quite weak
But there can be fun times ahead
If you only motivate yourself
Out of bed

PAUL HALLOWS

POEMS & A PLAY
WASTE

The mantra once was "Waste not, want not"
Now it's "Want it, get it, you deserve it".
It used to be "Make do and mend"
Now we throw away, what's not on trend.

Shoes used to be cherished, with Cherry Blossom
One pair for weekdays and one for Best, at most
Today we have trainers, boots made of leather
Wellies or sandals, to suit mood or weather

Spit in mascara to get the dried dredges
Makeup was precious and stretched out to last
Fingernail down lipstick, get into the edges
Not thrown away when the Sell-Buy date passed.

Older siblings' cast offs, not always good fit
Or jumble bought at the fayre
Hems turned up, let down, seams gathered in or let out
A stitch in time makes repair
Woolly jumpers carefully unravelled, re-knitted

Clothes washed, mended and more
altered, restyled, change a button, add a collar
Then cut up and used to make rugs for the floor

Before fridges and freezers bursting with food,
There were stone slabs in pantries to keep things fresh
Food on the plate, was eaten not left
Or go to bed hungry, don't complain, are you nesh

Milk was delivered to the door in glass bottles
Early each morning by milkmen on floats
Clean empty bottles collected, recycled
Not dropped in the streets, on the roads.

Now milk in plastic lasts much longer
Than in the glass bottles, on the stone slab
But discarded plastic, litters hedgerows and seas
It gets into the food chain and causes disease
And the scientists work against clock to cure cancer
Because we can't turn back the clock

The planet heats up and tsunamis destroy
This world where people forget how to walk
And how to say NO when they have enough
And landfills spill out with discarded stuff

And Santa brings toys, far more than is right
People get into debt they have no chance to clear
Father Christmas's sack then, was far lighter
But the Holiday season brought just as much cheer

Holidays once were a week by the sea
If you had enough money to spend
Or picking fruit on a farm in the sun
Now the world is your oyster to wend

You can sleep in a jungle, see Lions, Giraffe,
Or fly down a mountain on skis
Eat fondue with rock stars, as snow falls around
But please don't forget about bees

POEMS & A PLAY

Sail round the world, eat your fill of fine food,
Swim with the Sharks if you dare
Or walk along the Great Wall of China
See how the other folk fare.

Animals exploited then exported by sea
Force fed and injected to make profit
Caged in small pens to keep their meat lean
For spoiled human beings who think they deserve it.

So what of our children going on to the future
Rising water, hot climate, burnt trees
Is there time to stop it, perhaps, perhaps not
Listen to David Attenborough's pleas

So turn off the water,
And turn down the heat
Compost your peelings
The ozone replete

We worry about COVID, unemployment, education
But maybe this is as good as it gets
Let's do our bit, recycle our rubbish
Turn off the engine, lessen the threat.

VERONICA SCOTTON

THREE PEBBLES

© GRAHAM E WALKER

Walking over a lonely beach, leaving footprints in the sand
Looking down from the waters reach, three pebbles in my hand
Two thousand miles away from home, writing letters in my mind
Drawing pictures from my memory, just as if that I was blind

Chorus
I just want to see you again
I just want to hold you again
Walking down on them cobbled streets, whilst the rain is pouring down
Earning pennies for the family, whilst you're fighting for the crown
I sit before a tindered hearth, not knowing where you are
I cry myself to sleep at night, dreaming that you're not too far

Chorus

I think of times on the ship canal, and my home on Ordsall lane
The pubs that lined the Barbary Coast, they will never be the same
Our Sunday walks they made me smile, with the children hand in hand
What a difference here in purgatory, in this far off foreign land

Chorus

The time has passed so quick it seems, since we kissed beneath the moon
Your tears I captured in my heart then you went away too soon
My life it seems so empty now, as I watch our babies sleep
I know you're never coming back, but your love I'll always keep

Chorus x 2 then finish.

Copyright Graham E Walker Nov 2014

POEMS & A PLAY

THE LOAN SHARK

VERONICA SCOTTON

Writing Challenge:
The Friend of a Friend

CHILDREN PLAYING ON A PLAYGROUND, THEIR MOTHER SITTING ON A BENCH NEARBY

ACTORS: LEANNE, THE MOTHER.
FIONA, A FEMALE BYSTANDER
HARRY, THE LOANSHARK

KIDS	Mummy, The Ice Cream Man!
LEANNE	Sorry, not today.
KIDS	Aw, Why not?
LEANNE	No spare pennies today.
KIDS	OK
FIONA	What sweet kids, no tantrums.
LEANNE	They are great kids! And I feel so guilty, this is usually the 'once a week treat' that I can usually stretch too.
FIONA	Here's a fiver, go and get them an ice cream.
LEANNE	Thanks very much, how generous, but I don't know you, I couldn't possibly take your money. Once this virus goes away, I can get my job back and make it up to them.
LEANNE	Come on kids, time to go. We can pick some veg from out of the garden and you can help me to make soup.
FIONA	I'll walk along with you! You live near the launderette, don't you?
LEANNE	Yes, How do you know that?
FIONA	Oh, I've seen you around, I saw you taking your kids to school, you were walking with my friend Aimee and her little boy Jack. I was just putting my clothes in the dryer, when you walked past. I'll tell you what, let me join you for soup, and I'll bring a dessert.

KIDS   Yesss. Can we have yoghurt?

LEANNE   That would be lovely, but my husband is home. He came off his motorbike a couple of weeks ago and was quite badly injured. He doesn't like me bringing friends home to see him while he's laid up. Another time perhaps?

FIONA   Oh goodness, you are having it bad, aren't you. You are a saint you know. Look, my name's Fiona, here's my mobile number. If you fancy a coffee anytime, I could meet you in Costa.

LEANNE   That would be nice. I'm Leanne, lovely to meet you.

ONE WEEK LATER.

HUSBAND ON CRUTCHES COMPLAINING ABOUT DAYTIME TV. LEANNE LEAVES THE WASHING UP, PICKS UP PHONE AND CALLS.

LEANNE   Hi Fiona, I thought I'd take you up on your invitation. I could do with some adult conversation. If you are free for a chat. I could meet you at Corner Café in half an hour. I can't afford Costa prices.

FIONA   Hi Leanne. I was just thinking about you, how have you been? How are the kids? Don't answer, I'll see you in half an hour, my treat.

HALF AN HOUR LATER, IN THE CAFÉ

LEANNE   I've had an awful week. Mike's fracture isn't healing as it should, he's taking it out on me and the kids. He doesn't want to acknowledge that we used to have two wages coming in, all be it that mine was zero hours contract. He's blaming our soup-or-beans-on-toast diet on his inability to heal. He's critical of me giving Bobby a haircut, saying I should have taken him to the barber. He says that he looks like nobody owns him.

FIONA   Typical chauvinistic man. He should appreciate you more. From what I've heard, you are a fantastic wife and mother Leanne, doing a great job in a difficult situation.

POEMS & A PLAY

LEANNE   Aw it's difficult for him, he's usually a fabulous husband and dad, I'm sure he would cope brilliantly if the roles were reversed. But it was the last straw this morning. The boiler has packed in, I had to boil a kettle for water so that the kids could have a wash before going to school. Good job we are not in the middle of winter.

FIONA   Oh no, it goes from bad to worse for you. How much will the boiler cost to fix?

LEANNE   Well, I phoned one of Mike's friends, he's a plumber. He seems to think it will be the thermostat. He could come around this evening to have a look, but it would cost about £200 to mend.

FIONA   Look, I've got some money in the bank. Interest rates are rubbish at the moment. Why don't you let me lend it to you. You could pay me back when you get your job back.

LEANNE   Put like that, it does make sense. I suppose it would be one less worry, one less thing for Mike to nag me about.

NEXT WEEK IN THE TWO WOMEN SIT OVER A COFFEE IN THE CORNER CAFÉ

FIONA   (AGITATED) Oh Leanne, I don't know how to tell you this. I'm not sure if I mentioned this, but my husband is in the army. Nasty piece of work he is. He's been checking up on me, and noticed the bank account is £200 down. I don't know why he is making such a fuss, but he's threatened what he is going to do to me if the money isn't returned to the bank, before he comes home on leave next week. I'm so scared. I'm sorry, but I need to ask you for the money back.

LEANNE   (UPSET AND ANGRY) But Fiona, you know there is no way that I can do that. Surely you must have known that this might happen. You've never mentioned a husband. And you practically forced me to take the money.

FIONA   (SELF-RIGHTEOUSLY) I can't believe that you are blaming me, after I've been such a good friend. I'm going to have to borrow the money. Could you manage £10 a week to cover the interest until you are in a position to pay back the whole amount?

10 WEEKS LATER
ON THE PHONE

LEANNE   Hi Fiona. It's coming up for Christmas and I really need to buy some stocking fillers for the kids. They will be disappointed that Father Christmas won't be leaving as much under the tree, as he did last year. I have paid you back £100 up to now. Can I leave the payments for the next two weeks? My mum always gives me £100 for Christmas, I can finish paying you with that on Boxing Day.

FIONA   Sorry Leanne, I think you've misunderstood. The £10 each week is just interest. You still owe £200 and if you don't pay for the next two weeks, then you will owe £220. Look, why don't I ask the guy that I borrowed from, to lend you another couple of hundred? You've managed to pay £10 each week, if you could find another £10, you would be able to give the kids the Christmas they deserve.

NEXT MORNING.
DOORBELL RINGS, LEANNE OPENS THE DOOR

MAN   Hiya Leanne, I presume?

LEANNE   Good morning, Do I know you?

MAN   I'm Harry, a friend of Fiona. I'm taking over collections.

LEANNE   (LOWERING VOICE) I don't understand, I am fine paying Fiona each week, I don't need someone to remind me.

HARRY   Well Darlin' this is how it's going to be. Your debt was £220, I understand. Another £200 at Christmas, plus my fee for taking on the debt, £20. That totals £440. You need to pay me £25 a week. £20 interest on the debt and £5 towards the money owed. I'll collect at the same time each week. Make sure you are in or the interest will accumulate.

ANECDOTES

RIPPED JEANS

PAUL HALLOWS

Writing Task:
Frank: Likes music
Obstacle: Ripped Jeans
Aim: To be young again
Action: Learn a new skill

Frank decided to have a stroll around the shops, daydreaming to be young again. Maybe he could wear some clothes that younger people are wearing, be it ripped jeans and trainers.

He didn't fancy tattoos or piercing of any kind.

Maybe he could listen to modern music, instead of Nat King Cole or similar. Maybe that would make him feel younger.

"What about if I styled my hair better?" thought Frank.

He decided to go into the shop. Going up to the counter he talked to the shop owner, Mrs Norris.

"I'm looking for something to make me look younger," Frank said nervously.

"Well," said Mrs Norris, "I don't think you are the type of person for my shop."

"How rude," exclaimed Frank, "I have as much right as anybody to voice my opinion."

"OK," replied the shop owner.

"Maybe I could see someone else with a better attitude or I may as well go to a different shop."

"OK. What are you looking for?"

"Maybe a change of clothes for starters. Young people seem to be wearing ripped jeans, T shirts and trainers. Maybe something like that."

"Well," said Mrs Norris, going over to the rail of clothes. "How about this Adidas T-shirt?"

"Yes," said Frank, "I quite like that. What size is it?"

"XXL"

"Mmm just my size. How much willl it be?"

"Ten pounds."

"Do you have any ripped jeans?"

"Yes over here."

She takes down a pair of blue jeans with rips from the shelf.

"Go on. Try them on."

Frank goes into the changing room, locks the door, changes his clothes and then comes out.

The clothes are far to small.

"Oh these won't do. I thought you said they were XXL. These are clearly marked wrong."

"So what are you going to do?" asks Mrs Norris.

"I'm going to forget this malarkey and learn to drive instead."

ANECDOTES
HAVE YOU GOT...?
Catherine Grant-Salmon

It's a busy Saturday morning on Swinton Precinct
Yes readers this is a historical anecdote.

I'm working at the Oxfam shop behind the counter and till
Serving and helping customers
As they try to barter 50p off an already cut-price bargain

Children browse among the toys, books, and tat.
Our regulars come in for a mooch and a chat.
I see that hasn't sold this week again, they say.
How long have you had it on display is remarked?

An ornament or brick a brack from someone's forgotten past.
So sad when families come in with Mum's loved treasures.
Now forgotten, death or a nursing home

Our assortment of books is our pride and joy.
Tenderly cared for by Bill
An old school gentleman with a twinkle in his eye

They are all kept in alphabetical order.
From Cookson, Patterson, Steele and Tolkien
Low and behold if you disrupted his organised system.

And so dear listeners
I've set the scene...

A lady comes in and quietly takes me to one side.
"Have you got any Mills and Boon?"
Then hesitates – they are for my mother.
You'd think that she was asking for porn.

"No, I say" with regret.
"Would she like a bonk buster by Jackie Collins or
A Murder Mystery"
"Oh no, she likes Mills and Boon."
The escapism reading about a love struck enchanting virgin
Beautiful and innocent

The handsome caddish mysterious exotic man
Who whisks her away to a foreign land
Tempting her with his touch

And so, we both think about these stories.
The rambling hills of Tuscany or
The Savannah plain
Where these are always set
Instead of being stuck in Swinton
On another boring day

Just wait a minute …
Can we just escape for a moment?

Bill pops his head around
"I've found the one you wanted after all."
Hidden amongst all the tat
Forgotten not at all.

ANECDOTES
MATHEMATICAL EVOLUTION

COLIN BALMER

Writing Challenge:

Integrate all the cubes into a short story

'2b or not 2b? That is the question...' Mr Jenkins, head of mathematics at St Dumbell's Academy, had the onerous challenge of introducing the Lower Fourth to differentiation on his 'Calculus for Learners' course.

'... and it's nothing to do with a quotation from Hamlet.'

Sometimes, he thought, this lot had no more intelligence than when man first dropped out of the tree. In consolation he felt the more advanced had at least the ability to hold an abacus upright.

Roberts minor seldom spoke, but here was in his element.

He put up his hand. 'Please Sir, As the derivative of x squared is 2x, therefore the derivative of b squared will be 2b, Sir! QED.'

'Thank you, Roberts. Our arrow of learning is pointing forwards again.' Mr Jenkins said as he rubber-stamped a smiley face emoji on the youngster's progress chart.

GLASS HOUSES

COLIN BALMER

> People in glass houses are the metaphoric critics who will denigrate others without looking to their own faults. I suggest the provenance of the metaphor is similarly questionable.

Miserable Henry lived in a glass house like all the other people in Glass Street. Unlike his neighbours, however, he did not live by the clichéd maxim 'people in glass house should not throw stones.' He would scatter his metaphorical stones left, right and centre criticising anyone and anything that he felt did not fit neatly into his own way of looking at the world. If his habit were to wash the car after rain, he'd chastise Bert next door for wasting water by washing his in sunshine. If Henry felt it best to cut the grass in the morning he would be down on Tommy for noisily mowing on a Sunday afternoon. Nobody was spared his wrath and the frequent response was a shower of real stones though his glass windows, walls and doors. Their retaliation did nothing to change Henry's censure of other Glass Street dwellers. Children deliberately played football outside his house and looked forward to getting a tongue lashing from Henry. They knew they could torment him, with impunity from parental repercussion as they chucked pebbles through his panes. Those who lived on Glass Street sometimes felt as if Henry was prompting these rock fusillades.

After many years of Henry's reproach, the street noticed that the community had grown closer together. Sunday afternoons were quiet and peaceful. When the sun shone friends would gather for garden picnics. All lawns were mown simultaneously as were cars washed – or not at all. A park had been created where kids could play together.

The neighbourhood that had united against Henry felt no further need to throw stones – he had nothing to complain about – but above all he had invented, evaluated and installed toughened glass throughout.

People in glass houses may throw stones.

.

MEMORIES
RASPUTIN. SIR!

Paul Hallows

At high school I had a history teacher called Mr Richmond. He was very tall with short black hair and always wore a suit.

One day the inspectors were in his class. You could tell he was getting nervous.

He asked a question to the class.

"We have been learning about Russian monk. Can anyone tell me his name?"

Everyone was quiet. You could hear a pin drop. You could see the sweat pouring off him.

"Come on," he said, "Someone must know"

I put my hand up in the air.

"Paul knows, Sir," one of the lads shouted

"Ok Paul, what is it?"

I think he thought I needed the toilet or something.

"Rasputin. Sir!" I answered.

"Thank you Paul," he replied and carried on with the lesson.

After school, my mum, who was a school cleaner, was cleaning his room.

He told her the story and said,"When he gets older I will buy that lad a pint."

I'm still waiting for the pint.

ONCE UPON A TIME IN SALFORD

Ordsal Park, Number 8 dock gates,
Ships' crews clearing breakfast plates.
Buses with workers going to MetroVicks,
Roy Rogers on the Boro flicks
Taxi drives from the boozy Clowes
Dockers with cardboard in their shoes.
Ladies of the night 'giving their permission'.
Behind the Broadway and Central Mission.
Green and cream buses and Austin cars,
The Ship hotel and Cross Lane bars

Once Upon a Time in Salford

Wally Killen's chips that fed the masses,
Clean underwear from George Glass's
Old prams in the coke yard queue
A glass of Wilson's mild for me and you
Dancing nightly on Regent Road,
in the 'Cad' and people of no fixed abode
All nationalities in the Fox Inn
punch ups later, what a din.

Once Upon a Time in Salford

MEMORIES

Rowdy drunks on Saturday night
Telegraph wires festooned with kids' kites,
Cobbled streets, horse manure,
Rent collectors, faces sore
Kids playing hopscotch and ticky-it
Dirty-faced men from down the pit.
Sunshine in August, hazy November.
Scenes in Salford I remember
Cows running scared up the old Cross Lane,
Pushed into pens, never again.
Bonfire night – old chairs piled high,
Misty dream-like for all kids nearby.
I saw Graham Nash and Alan Clarke in the Direct Works club
Making their mark for future stardom,
Just for three quid each

Once Upon a Time in Salford

BERNIE SHAW

LIFE'S BETTER ON A HOUSEBOAT

ROSEMARY SWIFT

| Writing Challenge: |
| Picked from magazine snippets |

Toot, toot went Toad as he chugged along the river bank.

Looking every bit the image of a rustic bargeman, ruddy brown, complete with flat cap (but not cotton cloth tied around his neck), my younger brother Steve was thoroughly enjoying retirement as he manoeuvred his narrow boat along the canals of England. My family and I would hop on board when he pulled into Worsley near the Courthouse.

After spending years around the British Isles promoting Pedigree Chum at dog shows (more of a holiday than a job as he loves animals) followed by many more years trucking around Europe (going to Beer Festivals to show at what temperature Guinness should be served) and then not so pleasurable spending the last few years of his working life taking loads to either Gatwick or Heathrow airports, life for Steve had become idyllic.

His wife Maura would join Steve whenever she could but she was seeing out her last years of employment (by choice). Extended family would often be invited to their home in Hayfield Village for sumptuous festive lunches; whatever Maura tackled she did well – very much cordon bleu level when it came to cooking. In would go cream and butter to enhance taste.

Extremely active in village life and pencil-slim and fit through climbing Kinder Scout, what she did not realise was that her cholesterol had become sky high. Unfortunately, a 'Well Woman' appointment was postponed because of heavy snows and not being able to get out of the Village. A fresh appointment was made but not until after she had fitted in a break with Steve on the narrow boat.

Weaving in and out of backwaters of Yorkshire and then heading back to their Lancashire base, Maura suffered a major stroke in the middle of the night. Medical help eventually arrived but too late for her to be helped initially from a lot of the symptoms. From a backwater Yorkshire Hospital, Maura was transferred to Stepping

MEMORIES

Hill, Stockport where she lay incapacitated for many months. Since then has been cared for at home until sadly within the last few months she has been transferred to a nursing home with signs of dementia.

Ominously, I recall my cousin Christine inhaling deeply because my brother Steve had changed the name of the narrow boat to 'Hobson's Choice' (Hobson being his surname and indeed mine before marriage). Apparently it is extremely unlucky to rename a boat if failing to advise the deities that rule the elements; to counteract, there is an official boat naming ceremony that allows you to notify the powers that be and keep things right with the universe but doubt this was done by my brother Steve.

Superstition or not, my brother's life has been dramatically changed these past years, much more so for his wife Maura.

CORINTHIAN LADIES

ROSEMARY SWIFT

On 6 October 2023, Granada News and BBC Look North News reported on a mural and plaque being erected in Fog Lane Park, Didsbury in honour of the Manchester Corinthians Women's Football Team of the 1950s & 1960s. A full page article on page 3 of the Manchester Evening News on the same topic appeared the next day. Coincidentally on page 2 were tributes to Lady Cathy Ferguson, recently deceased, the wife of Sir Alex Ferguson, former Manager of Manchester United Football Club.

Fog Lane Park was the home ground of the Corinthians Ladies and their many trophies from almost instant success were displayed in the window of the fish & chip shop on Fog Lane. They did not have changing rooms and were said to bathe in the nearby duck pond in the park.

The football pitches on Parrs Wood Road side of the park were diagonally across from my home. At the park's far side were tennis courts (nine pence fee for a serious game on hard ground and four pence for a game on grass). Nearby said duck pond there was a pets' corner where peacocks screamed. My dad coming home in the early hours from regular nights at GPO Parcel Post hated their calls carrying over the misty fields as it reminded him of a baby crying. In clear view of our lounge window many a men's game of football took place on a weekly basis with a few onlookers. However, when the Corinthian Ladies played there were lots of spectators. Those travelling on the upper deck of the no. 74 bus that traversed between Manchester and Stockport could be seen craning their necks.

Manchester Corinthians had been founded in 1949 by Percy Ashley, principally so his daughter Doris could play. This was at a time when women were banned from playing on FA affiliated grounds. He chose the team name in homage to Corinthian FC, London's men's amateur football team famous for their sporting ideals. In time, Percy Ashley founded a second eleven named the Nomads.

MEMORIES

The Corinthians toured Portugal in 1957, following which they competed in a European Ladies Football Cup beating a German team. For that game their interpreter was Bert Trautmann, Manchester's City's iconic former goalkeeper. The Corinthians went on to enter many competitions, the longest being twelve weeks around South America and Caribbean in 1960; some of those matches attracted crowds of tens of thousands and much money was raised for charities.

Following Percy Ashley's death in 1967 the team was eclipsed by newer clubs but not before it had won the first Deal International Tournament (1968) and took part in an international tournament in Reims (1970) beating ACF Juventus 1–0 in the final.

[The 'Deal International' was a women's football competition founded by Arthur Hobbs, a carpenter with Deal Town Council. Possessed of great energy and focus, Hobbs became the founder of women's football in England, pioneering summer football for women more than 40 years before the FA WSL. In fact, before that, in 1917, women workers at Dick, Kerr & Company Munitions Factory in Preston formed a football team which soon became popular; playing other sides around the country which led to becoming one of the most successful ladies football sides worldwide helping to pave the way for the modern game.]

The Corinthians also won the Women's Football Association's (WFA) Teddy Gray Memorial Challenge Trophy in 1968 & 1969 but lost in the 1970 final. They were one of 44 clubs represented at WFA's inaugural AGM at Caxton Hall.

Full praise to the recent successes of England's Women's Football Team, winners of European Cup (2022) and runners-up in World Cup (2023) and well done to the present crop of women who are playing for prestigious British Clubs but let us not forget forerunners such Dick, Kerr Ladies and Corinthians Ladies.

MUSIC AND DANCE WITH DEMENTIA

Chris Vickers

On his Sunday morning show in September Phil Trow of BBC Radio interviewed Lesley Fisher who founded the Dancing with Dementia local charity for people living with dementia, their family, friends and carers. The 'family'.

When Lesley's sister developed vascular dementia in 2014 there was no guidance, assistance or support offered leaving her feeling isolated and alone. However, Lesley pushed back and researched the condition and found a study conducted in the USA in 1948 which recommended music and dancing as proven therapies. Through friends Lesley was made aware of a Singing with Dementia group at the Humphrey Booth Centre in Swinton which proved to be an excellent conduit to meet like-minded people and she offered her support.

As it happened Swinton's Grand Palais, built in 1912 and a longstanding community hub was to reopen after major refurbishment with a beautiful sprung floor ballroom offering a place where many family members had attended years before for ballroom dance classes, courting or witnessing local and international stars when it later became the Wishing Well club.

Determined to use this iconic landmark Lesley asked two friends to join her and received a £300 Start-Up grant from the Swinton Health Improvement Team. Dancing with Dementia was born with the first event being in February 2016 with twenty-four guests. The early months proved so challenging that the enterprise almost failed until Lesley was told: 'I told you it would never work!' Galvanised by this slight she held meetings with local care home activity coordinators and heeded their advice. Live artists were booked and social events created, with a licensed bar on Monday afternoons enabling people to attend and get home before dark. Guests responded and turned up in their droves to enjoy the music, dance and reminisce, with pre-pandemic numbers of up to one hundred and eighty.

MEMORIES

Meanwhile, in September 2021, ninety-two year old June Smith who had set up Singing with Dementia at Humphrey Booth in late 2015 passed on the baton to Lesley and her colleagues, with a donation to the cause also. Under their stewardship the organisation has truly blossomed.

I attended a session with photographer Paul Sherlock arriving early as guests arrived, each given a chit to claim a tea or coffee from the Forget Me Not café, some people also enjoying lunch there too. We were warmly welcomed by Jeanette Cutt, the group's treasurer and an immaculate, upbeat octogenarian named Donald Carr self-proclaimed 'meeter and greeter'. Donald being one of the many volunteers and supporters who freely give their time to help out. As the 'family' gathered, sipped drinks and chatted away performer Tony Mack set up his equipment before launching into his act at eleven o'clock and by song two (Elvis) it seemed that virtually everyone was up and dancing…smiling, carefree, 'leaving the dementia at home.' The feel good factor was palpable, 'not what you expected was it?' Lesley asked me and it really wasn't.

I was introduced to another Lesley, a Wellbeing Coordinator from Pendleton Court care home who had brought guests and who was effusive in her praise of the trustees, 'during the pandemic we were completely isolated but received help from this group in the form of PPE equipment, which was hard to get, treats of sweets, cakes and toiletries, which were for residents and staff alike. We made lasting friendships from that time.'

The pandemic forced the group to diversify and liaise with various funding organisations such as CVS, with whom they worked with a local café and delivered lunches to private homes, before upscaling with extra funding via Forever Manchester and sending out over four hundred plus meals. The success of Music and Dance with Dementia is down to a dedicated team who listen to guests needs 'never forgetting the me in dementia' and who as a small charity can move on projects quickly and with passion to drive them forward. Their innovations include: the Baby Love initiative whereby dolls are received in care homes for guests to look after, with knitted clothing and cot bedding also provided; the Birthday Box which provides a gift and card to recognise birthdays; telephone buddies where groups of up to ten guests contact each other weekly to maintain contact; numerous Days Out to Blackpool's Tower Ballroom or the Illuminations or a Christmas trip to a historic house with afternoon tea, singing festive songs in a candlelit music room with mulled wine, among many other initiatives.

The achievements are immense and all credit to the Trustees for their dedication and hard work: Lesley Fisher, Jeanette Cutt, Elaine Fox, Ann Bellis and Betty Burton… 'ordinary people doing extraordinary things indeed.'

MEMORIES

From the Dancing with Dementia flyer: at the time of printing.

Dancing with Dementia

"WHO WE ARE"

DANCING WITH DEMENTIA IS A LOCAL CHARITY FOR PEOPLE LIVING WITH DEMENTIA, THEIR FAMILIES, FRIENDS, AND CARERS.

During the pandemic caring for a loved one living with dementia has been challenging at best and harrowing at worst. In a non-clinical venue, we provide a place where people living with dementia, their family, friends and carers can share social activities. Creating a place where other guests con offer support and empathy with the situation.

We create a welcoming and uplifting atmosphere by inviting professional artists to perform music and song which will both rekindle memories and stimulate conversations for our guests. Meeting up with family and friends and sharing in light refreshments creates a sense of wellbeing for all.

By being included in social activity there is re-connection with the community and a sense of belonging and being valued.

We meet at The Grand Palais, Station Rood Swinton, M27 6AH on the second Monday in the month 1.00pm until 3.00pm

This is a free event – (we do appreciate donations!) A free hot drink and light refreshments are available.

We are entertained by professional artist in a beautiful ballroom. There is a licensed bar where soft drinks and stronger may be purchased.

Our guests are encouraged to sing along to the popular songs of their era and even to venture onto the dance floor and enjoy the dancing or chatting to friends and making new friends!

We also hold a raffle to add fun and additional joy to the event.

Initially the sessions were for people living with dementia, their family friends and carers. After some research we found that isolation, loneliness and depression can be contributory factors to the condition. With that information it was decided that we would open our doors to anyone who felt low in spirit and address the needs and increase the wellbeing of the senior citizens in the community.

WHERE ARE THEY?

Lorraine Tattersall

Pans waiting on the hob, cupboard doors opening and closing, as all the ingredients needed to make the tea were taken out and waiting to be mixed together and placed in those pans. The cookery book removed from the kitchen drawer, its pages covered in fingerprints from previous meals.

"Oh, dear, where are my glasses," Maureen muttered looking around the disorganised worktops, before lifting and moving things around to see if her glasses had got hidden among the items but no such luck.

Tapping her lips with her fingers, she thought about when and where she last had them, so going from the kitchen back to the living room the book she was reading earlier was still on the side table where she had left it, having decided to finish off the chapter she was halfway through before going to make the tea but, no, they weren't there either. She looked behind the cushions, then down the side of the settee, now on her hands and knees looking under the settee.

Her husband Robert looked up from the newspaper from which he was trying to pick out some winners from the list of dogs that were running at tonight's meeting and watched his wife's actions before going back to his reading. He had given up thinking and often wondered why women in general acted so strangely.

Playing a game, in a world of his own, on his Play Station, her son Andrew was on the other settee. Maureen watched as his fingers moved a hundred miles an hour and his tongue lolling out of his mouth as he tried desperately to alienate the ball of flames heading his way from his game. So it was no using asking him, she thought, even if the house was on fire nothing would deter him.

Robert continued to scrutinise the runners, picking out the winner was an art in itself, and looking at the form of each dog's previous run could potentially make him an extra few bob but his wife's lifting and moving things around was putting him off. He was sorry

MEMORIES

now he hadn't gone to the bookies where he would have had more peace. But watching his wife getting more and more agitated and muttering to herself he lifted the paper higher so she couldn't see the expression on his face and how he was struggling not to laugh.

Once more, Maureen was active – this time bounding up the stairs. Robert could hear drawers opening, the squeak of the wardrobe door meant she was looking in there too. Footsteps were heard coming from the stairs and his wife was back in the living room.

"What's up, love?" Robert asked.

"What's up?" she replied "I've lost my glasses, that's what up and you two are a waste of time. You know I can't function without my glasses and all you think about is your damn dogs."

"And as for you" she shouted, pointing to her son absorbed in his game, "..well, I've had enough, I'm off to the chip shop when it opens, you two can sort your own teas out."

Andrew took off his headphones; he'd not seen his mum like this before.

"What's up, Mum?" he asked.

"I've lost my glasses" she replied "if I stood on my head in the corner you two would take no notice."

Frowning, Andrew turned to his dad wondering what his mum was going on about. Robert folded his paper and placed it on his knees before saying.

"Oh, I wouldn't do that love, you will break your glasses."

Maureen was gobsmacked as she put her hand on the top of her head to find her glasses there. She placed them back on, turned her nose up in the air and went back to finish making the tea.

Andrew resumed his game and Robert continued to study the form of the dogs shaking his head, saying,"Women!"

Other Publications by SWit'CH

My Life and Other Misadventures   ISBN 978-1-326-60665-7
Alan Rick
A collection of humorous and poignant nostalgic reminiscences covering Alan's early school years in the war to national service in Egypt. Alan looks askance at the society of the day with a wry, knowing, smile.

Switch On, Write On, Read On   ISBN 978-1-326-73048-2
Approx. 200 page the first showcase of the group's creativity. Containing nearly sixty humorous, whimsical, thought-provoking, ironic, and eclectic writing.

A Write Good Read   ISBN 978-0-244-73623-1
Tales from Swinton and Salford; the Wigan train and around the world drawing on the experiences and interests of the group. Modern telecoms and IT feature, so do the Ten Commandments and seven dwarfs. Historical pieces range from the industrial revolution to individual childhood memories.

Peterloo People   ISBN 978-0-244-18472-8
A potpourri of passions gives the reader the chance to walk in those shoes to the peaceful protest, the actions on the day and shameful reaction afterwards. But the focus is not only on the victims; the perspectives of the authorities and militia are treated with sympathy and criticism in due turn – and there's even a wry tale of hope and salvation for a pariah in the guise of a government spy.

The Taste of Teardrops   ISBN 978-0-244-26569-4
A Novel by Judith Barrie.
A gripping psychological thriller set in a sleepy seaside town. It's 1981 and a young woman settles into her cosy new home believing that she had found peace and tranquillity after a painful marriage break-up. But there are mysteries. Who is the woman upstairs and the irresistibly attractive man who visits her?

Memories Unlocked   ISBN 9798570919617
These childhood reminiscences of localities now gone, holidays, school, nature notes, plane crashes, sex education and walking home after dancing form part of the mischief, mayhem and misadventures of our young lives. Drawn from the experiences of SWit'CH writers in their formative years.

Selected Memories   ISBN 9798598323212
This choice of writers' recollections taken from Memories Unlocked follows on from The Big Switch, which was produced for those with a visual impairment, with a font developed by RNIB. The book is easy to handle. Big letters on low contrast paper make it an easy read and a 'page turner' in the literal sense.

War and Peace in Pludde Bailey   ISBN 979-8391352990
A Novel by Judith Barrie
Pludde Bailey an old fashioned village. There was a public house where men gathered to argue; a corbner shop where the women gathered to gossip; a quaint little chiurch up on the hill. Occupied with blackout curtains, rationing and air raid shelters, not one of the inhabitants suspected that they harboured a fledgling killer or that he would kill again nearly twenty years later.

The Big Switch   ISBN : 9798644090433
A collection of short stories in large print format for readers with a visual impairment such as Macular Degeneration or Glaucoma.
'The Big Switch' is a compilation of extracts from some of the group's previously published works. Designed for easy reading.

A Pain in the Bum   ISBN: 9798590032099
Veronica Scotton
The author's words say it all "I was so very fortunate, not to have to face my cancer alone. Whenever I began to feel overwhelmed, the rock who is my husband was by my side. My children and grandchildren lifted my spirits by being positive about the whole thing and my siblings and friends with their humour, often black humour gave me the best medicine."

Time of the Virus.   ISBN: 9798541841855
Sylvia Edwards
Is what IS how it must always be? Let's make our world a better place. Complemented by poems, stories and artwork, this book debates key issues, eg. racism, religion, politics.

A Lie Never Dies.   ISBN: 979-8387509599
A Novel Sylvia Edwards
1901. This novel charts the dramatic consequences of a lie that drags Kristina through a maze of emotional challenges, changing her life forever. Can she find lasting happiness ina world where she does not belong?

All Kinds of Everything   ISBN 9798371732019
A collection from the 2023 team of writers. Stories and poetry complemented by members reminiscences. As new members join us, our versatility and variations expand. This collection compares well with the standards established and maintained over the years of the group's successes.

How Times Have Changed!   ISBN: 9798877331617
Sylvia Edwards
These memoirs attempt to bridge the post-WW2 world with today's technological version. Yet, in 2024, as wars still rage, I wonder if humanity is any different than it was - or ever will be. Against this backdrop, I have told my personal story with honesty and sincerity and hope that my version of truth reflects what was.